THE
BONE
WAY

By Holly J. Underhill

Copyright Notice

Cover art by Claudia Caranfa
Editing by Celine Frohn
Back cover & typesetting by Charlie Bramald

ISBN 978-1-9163669-6-1 (paperback)
ISBN 978-1-9163669-5-4 (ebook)

Published by Nyx Publishing
Sheffield, United Kingdom 2021
www.nyxpublishing.com

 NYX PUBLISHING

For the ones I've lost,
I would have traveled the Bone Way for you

PART ONE

Chapter One

Teagan couldn't find her favorite ritual dagger. The one her mother had given her when she was a young girl ready to begin her training as a witch, the one with the star-engraved handle and a blade that had a shine to it like the world's darkest midnight. *You are being entrusted with this, do not lose it. It is not a toy. It is your gift to carry forever.* But she'd lost it.

Teagan cursed and threw her hands up in exasperation. She'd searched the house thoroughly after she'd found Cress's note earlier this morning; the kitchen overflowing with potted plants and the scents of basil and freshly-baked bread, the den filled with lived-in furniture, the bedroom with its soft four-poster bed and windows overlooking the garden, and even the root cellar where they stored food and wine. Their house had always felt cozy and safe, but now it felt empty and desolate without Cress.

Her wife was gone, and her dagger too, and she didn't know if she'd ever see either again. As she looked around the den, she was struck with the sudden surety that Cressidae had taken it. She had taken it with her to the Shadow Realm. Of course, she would have. She'd never known a person so stubborn or angry when she was told no. That woman loved her with all of that hotheaded loyalty and more.

Sometimes Teagan wondered if she was even worth all that.

Teagan knew she was running out of time to catch up with Cress, knew she still had one last errand to run before she could pursue her. But she paused for a moment in the silence, inhaling the lingering scent of Cress's favorite lavender perfume, and wondered if she'd see this place again. It was the home Teagan had grown up in and inherited four years ago after her mother passed. She'd spent half of that time living at the Wystira Academy in the city of Tyras, but that was before she'd met Cress and everything had changed. They'd moved back after Teagan got hurt, and she'd been happy to leave the crowds behind, to settle into the house that had been in her mother's family for generations.

Their cats, Elra and Ohlia, twined around her legs, and she leaned down to scratch beneath their chins and kiss them goodbye before she grabbed her bag. Cress had packed everything for her, when they'd still planned to travel the Bone Way together, before they'd fought and Cress took off without warning. The bag sat heavily on her shoulders, a constant reminder of their argument.

It was a little unsettling to walk the dirt road that led into Lefora, a small town in the southern regions of Wystira, without Cress beside her. They had walked this path together countless times, pushing so close there was never any space between them. Their neighbors were mostly farmers, and the farms were spaced apart, popping in and out of densely-packed trees.

She waved to other folks but kept her head down so they wouldn't feel the need to chat. She breathed with relief when she got to the healer's shop, where she was immediately surrounded by comfort and the smell of the harmona herb, a woodsy and smoky aroma. A fire burned low in a grate on the far wall, warming her cold hands. They seemed to always be cold nowadays.

Maradin didn't glance up from her work. "I was wondering when I'd see you in here."

Her hair was bound up at the nape of her neck, and Teagan saw wisps of gray between the black strands as Maradin continued grinding herbs together for tea. The healer witch was in her late fifties, with a sharp keenness about her. Teagan had to keep this exchange short. "I need the coranderis petals, crushed."

They'd had most of the ingredients at home, for a witch was always prepared. Teagan had also packed ones that wouldn't really help her but might bring her comfort on the journey. But according to Cress's research, they needed the dust of crushed coranderis petals. They'd saved getting that for last so Maradin—who had an encyclopedic knowledge of herbs and their uses—wouldn't know what they were planning to do until it was too late to stop them.

"It's funny," Maradin said. "Cressidae stopped by this morning, askin' for the same thing."

Teagan didn't say anything for a moment, not out of shame but respect. Maradin had known Teagan's family for a long time, and when Teagan lost her mother, Maradin stepped in. She was the one who'd checked in on the girl, taught her how to clear her mind and create a space for herself. The house had been too lonely, too *empty*, and Teagan couldn't exist inside it without feeling weighed down with grief and despair. But homes could be cleared just as minds could be, and she'd gone through the rooms with peaceful intent and a spell, waving away the fog that hung over everything. And in time, she'd come to know it as *hers*.

Hers and Cressidae's.

"I can't stay long," Teagan said.

Maradin set a bottle in front of Teagan and pursed her lips. "Don't make me regret tellin' the two of you the truth about the Shadow Princess. That creature came from her realm, but it doesn't mean she'll help you even if you survive long enough to find her."

When Teagan didn't answer, Maradin said, "Goddess go with you." Teagan smiled thinly, appreciative of the blessing. Like many witches, she had been brought up in the faith and continued to keep it, though it had been hard at times. The Goddess, it was said, had once saved Wystira from the rising darkness many centuries ago. Why hadn't the Goddess saved her from the darkness of losing her mother? She had been so angry and lonely that she'd lost some of her faith. Grief never truly heals, but faith can offer solace, and Teagan wished it had offered her more than that.

"If we don't come back, will you take care of Elra and Ohlia?" She'd made sure the cats had enough food and water for at least a week, but there was always the possibility they wouldn't make it home. She tried not to think about that, though.

"Of course."

"I'll see you soon, Maradin." Maybe if she said that out loud, and with confidence, she'd make the promise come true.

"Be careful," Maradin called out before Teagan left. "The Shadow Princess isn't known for honest deals."

After Teagan closed the door behind her, she knelt on the front step to put the bottle in her pack. Something white fluttered out between her herbs and a scarf. Teagan grabbed for it and held it up; the note had only two words on it.

I'm sorry.

Teagan shredded it to pieces and shouldered the bag as she started down the road again, leaving Lefora behind.

The Hallowed Arch stood on a cliff overlooking the sea that

surrounded much of Wystira, and it didn't take long to reach it. There were other arches around the country, other places to enter the Shadow Realm, but this was the closest one. She had always thought the story of the Shadow Princess and her Deathly Palace was simply that: a story. A tall tale that parents told their children to get them to sleep. Even though her own mother had used it as a lullaby, and mentioned time and time again how one day Teagan might have need to travel the Road of Silence, she hadn't truly believed it.

Not until the day she'd come across that creature, the grisleck, in the Asoria Forest.

Teagan's hand strayed to her bandaged left arm, felt the echoes of the monster biting into her, and shook free of the terrible memory. She squared her shoulders and faced the stone arch, lone and tall and brimming with power. A salty sea breeze swept her hair around her face, so she pulled it up into a high ponytail with shaking fingers. This structure was *ancient*, and she could feel it in her bones as she walked closer to it. It'd always been here, its history forgotten. She remembered being dared to get close to it by the girl she'd liked and was trying to impress when she was younger. She remembered the power she felt from it then, and it had scared her. But now that she understood, she was less fearful.

Teagan pulled Cress's bound notebook from her pack, the pages nearly spilling out of it. It held all of Cress's research about the Shadow Realm and its ruler; every piece of information they could find in the dusty shelves of libraries. She ran her fingers over Cress's handwriting, the drawings she'd made in the margins, translations of the elegant calligraphy engraved in stone in a language almost-forgotten. The only traces left behind when the legend of the princess and her kingdom of the dead became a myth.

The arch stood at the very edge of the cliff; there was nowhere to go but down. *Keep your thoughts close and your heart strong, for one false step could mean certain death.* It was a leap of faith, a leap of courage. Teagan imagined if you didn't have enough faith and courage, you'd simply fall to your death, smacking your head on the rocks and bleeding out below the waves. You didn't reach the Deathly Palace if you weren't fueled by daring ambition and a strong sense of yourself. But standing at the cliff's edge and seeing the waves throw themselves at the rocky coast so far below, Teagan faltered. This was a lot to ask for one who'd only just learned the Shadow Realm was real last month, who still wasn't even sure this was worth it. The reason she'd fought with Cress, the reason they were separated now, was because Teagan hadn't wanted to put Cress's life on the line too. The Road of Silence was dangerous, and the Princess even more so. If Cress got hurt, or worse, then this would all be for nothing. They'd argued until they couldn't anymore; Cress wouldn't be persuaded otherwise and Teagan was too exhausted to keep pushing it.

So she'd woken up alone, her pack at the door with a two-word note inside.

"You should have waited for me, Cress." Teagan sighed and wished it hadn't gone this way, wished she didn't feel responsible for whatever happened to Cress. She put the book away and strode forward. She couldn't just leave Cress to battle alone. Teagan had all her research; she'd make it through the Bone Way and beyond.

She'd reach the Desolate Mountain if she was careful. If she was surefooted and strong of heart, she'd be at the Deathly Palace in a few days' time. And when she got there, she'd find Cress and drag her home.

Her resolve strengthened; she trusted Cress and she'd follow her wife anywhere, even to almost certain death.

Teagan stepped through the archway and fell.

Two Years Ago

Teagan wove through the crowded sidewalks of Wystira's Academy. Her lectures were done for the day, and her head ached from all the information thrown her way. She didn't know if she'd ever get used to the course load. After her mother died, Teagan had decided to follow in her footsteps to become a healer witch and return to Lefora and put her own services to use. Lefora had Maradin already, but there was always room for more healers in a town.

Most of the people in Wystira were witches. Some were born with a particular affinity for the elements or accessing the spirit realm where Wystira's Goddess resided and ruled. Some, like Teagan's mother, used traditional means of healing as well as guidance from the Goddess and channeled energy from the spiritual plane. The Academy in Tyras, Wystira's capital, offered a wide range of studies, both of the magical and non-magical variety. The non-magical options included history, engineering, and art, among others.

Teagan's mother had firmly believed that witchery was for everyone, as long as they had good intentions. She'd always made sure Teagan knew the witch's path was a choice, even though she'd been brought up as a witch's daughter and it was the natural course of action to apprentice with her mother.

Teagan had wanted to pursue a different path when she was younger, to become a world-renowned inventor. But then her mother died and all she could think about was honoring the woman's life.

Still, she wished the classes would get easier.

Teagan had the rest of the day off, and she intended to leave her studies behind for a moment and visit the city's markets. Since she'd moved to Tyras and begun her classes, she hadn't had much time to herself. She'd preferred that, in the beginning, when the memories of her mother were still too close to the surface, but now she'd been here for almost four months and she'd hardly seen any of it. When she'd taken the steam-powered train into Tyras, she'd gone straight to the academy.

She soaked up her surroundings now as she made her way into the heart of the city. If Wystira was anything, it was the intersection of modernity and magic. This was a country founded on not just witchery, but innovation. Steam-powered engines cut through the countryside, decorating the landscape alongside forests and rivers and mountains. Machines flew through the air, balloons rose high above the city's tallest roofs, and carriages were no longer only pulled by horses. Inventions made everyday life easier, while magic kept the people connected to their Goddess. Kept them in health and heart and happiness. Though not everyone worshiped her anymore, most understood there was more to life than what they could see and hear and feel.

Teagan felt the magic all around her, the energy from spells that crackled through the noise, the scent of harmona in the air. In her small town, she'd lived so far apart from anyone else; she'd never experienced such an open display of witchery. Through a window in a cottage, she could see a pot being stirred on its own, while an invisible cook chopped vegetables. A street performer blew into their hands and a flock of butterflies burst from their palms to fly around those gathered to watch. Another read cards for those brave enough to seek out their fates. Teagan didn't like the cards; she preferred not knowing her future. She wanted to live every day as it came.

A part of her wondered if the knowing would help ease grief, when it was time, but she didn't think it was worth it.

A sudden gust of wind brought a chill, and Teagan wrapped her cloak tightly around herself. It was nearing winter, when fresh blankets of snow would cover the ground and the trees and the buildings. They got snow in Lefora, but not nearly as much as Tyras did, going by the stories from older students. She was almost looking forward to it, though she knew she'd resent the cold in time.

After Teagan turned a corner, she stood in an open square surrounded by shrubbery and flowers. It was a garden in the middle of the city, and it would have been out of place were it not for all the people gathered around. Couples and families had settled blankets on the open ground under the autumn sunlight, the shade the trees offered in summer no longer sought. Benches were spaced throughout the garden, and proud statues lined the path as she ventured further. The path led her to the centerpiece of the garden: a gigantic fountain depicting the Goddess.

The Goddess was shown as a young woman, with long hair braided with flowers and a smile on her face. Sometimes she was depicted without a smile, as if people wanted to remember her as the serious, powerful heroine who saved the world from darkness. In this sculptor's rendering, a star was also held upright in her open palms. "The star glows at night," a passerby remarked to their companion.

As Teagan looked around, she saw a goddess of her own. The woman to her right bit her lip and stared at an easel with a canvas in front of her, the fountain and garden drawn vividly in broad strokes of color. Teagan couldn't tear her eyes from her, and her staring must have drawn the woman from her concentration. She turned toward Teagan, paintbrush in hand, specks of color on her shirt and on her fingers. She didn't seem to mind the paint splatters. Her expression had been furrowed in concentration, but now it was cleared in friendly greeting. She

14

was stunning; long, golden hair and bright blue eyes, a top lip that was slightly larger than the bottom. There was also a very small, almost unnoticeable scar above her left eye. Teagan desperately wanted to know how she got that.

"Beautiful," Teagan breathed.

The woman beamed, looking at her artwork. "Thank you." Teagan hadn't been talking about the painting, though yes, it was beautiful as well. "Are you an artist too?"

"A healer, or I will be."

"Ah, a student of Wystira's fine academy, huh? Have you always lived here, or no—you've the look of someone seeing this garden for the first time. Where are you from originally?"

"Lefora," Teagan replied.

"I have not heard of Lefora."

Teagan went to say that it wasn't worth knowing, but that wasn't true. Lefora was simply overlooked except by those who loved it. "It's a wonderful little town in the south."

"Then I must visit someday."

"I'd gladly show you around." Even though there was nothing in Lefora to really show her. Teagan wanted to groan at her shaky flirtation skills. It'd been a while since she'd had the energy to spend on romantic relationships; she found she was nervous and worried she didn't know what to say anymore.

The woman smiled widely at her, and the nerves disappeared. "I'm Cress."

"Teagan."

"Well, Teagan, I'd gladly show *you* around Tyras, if you'd like." She grinned mischievously. "After all, it wouldn't be right for you to offer, and not myself."

Teagan nearly giggled at that, but she closed her mouth and simply nodded. Cress packed her things and led the way back into the city proper, Teagan following closely at her side. Cress showed Teagan her favorite markets and restaurants, places she would have never discovered on her own. They talked about anything and everything. Teagan felt so comfortable and safe with this woman that she found herself mentioning her mother and how much she missed her, why she was studying medicine at the academy. Cress spoke of art and the whirlwind of city life, of long nights spent in a creative daze. Teagan hung on every word from her lips, her attention never wavering. And when night fell, Teagan didn't want to go back to her dorm room—she wanted to stay in this moment, this day, with Cress.

Cress took her hand, threading their fingers together. Teagan's stomach fluttered at the touch, and she worried her palms would sweat. "There's a special spot I'd like to show you." Cress tugged her down more streets until they came to a large building that overshadowed everything else in its vicinity. "This is my family's home." Teagan worried at first; she'd only just met Cress and it was too soon to meet her family too. But Cress only took her through the house to get to the balcony in the back.

Teagan leaned against the iron-wrought balustrade in awe. Tyras was laid out before her, all shining lights and soft music and warm laughter. Teagan looked over, and Cress was staring at her, an intensity in her eyes that kindled a fire in Teagan.

"You're so beautiful. I want to paint you," Cress said, her voice soft and full of promise. Teagan wasn't sure about *beautiful*; she'd let her straight brown hair grow to her shoulders, her clothes were plain and worn, and her face was so thin, a hollowness that she didn't think made her look striking at all. Still, Teagan couldn't find it within herself to say no. She settled into her spot, her arms on the balcony and her face upturned toward the waxing crescent moon.

Cress smiled at her, so warm and lovely that it took her breath away. Teagan knew, even then, she'd follow that smile anywhere.

Chapter Two

Teagan fell. For an endless moment, she hung suspended in the air. The image of her broken body smashed on the rocks below the Hallowed Arch flashed before her eyes. She squeezed her eyes shut, her breath caught in her throat.

She fell, but it was not to her death. Or, well, it wasn't to the can-never-come-back-from-it kind of death. There was a swooping feeling in her stomach as she landed hard on her knees on cold ground. Despite the stinging pain in her knees, she was grateful for its familiar solidity. The air was chilly, and she rubbed her hands up and down her arms as she got to her feet. She looked around, and though she'd known going through the Bone Way was the first step, she couldn't help the gasp that slipped out at the sight.

What lay under her boots was a stone path that stretched into the distance as far as her eyes could see, but that wasn't what shocked her. There were bones *everywhere*. On either side of the path, broken fingers reached forward as if to grab her.

Skulls grinned lopsidedly at her; whole skeletons lay curled or sprawled out as if people had simply stepped off the Bone Way and laid themselves to rest. The sky was a clear, startling gray, a wall of dark slate no matter which way she turned. She wondered if Cress's hands had itched to grab a pencil, to render the Bone Way alive in the way it was now, as Cress could do with all of her drawings. The sight was amazingly morbid. Those who didn't make it through this part of the realm never left it; it was impossible to count how many had died here, lost in a forgotten kingdom. More souls for the Shadow Princess's collection.

A clattering drew her attention. Was someone else here? *Cress*? Something moved in the corner of her eye, and Teagan whipped her head towards the motion, but saw only the silent white teeth of a pile of skulls. She almost screamed when the bones nearby shifted. It was only a small unfurling of a finger, a hand. Teagan felt shaky as the skeleton lifted itself from the ground. Then it was moving *toward* her, moaning from unhinged jaws and crawling forward on what was left of its limbs. All around her, the other bones started to rattle. Teagan scrabbled back in horror and swung her pack around so she could reach inside it. Her heart beat furiously as the clacking of the bones grew louder. She rummaged in her pack, panic building as more skeletons clattered to their feet and lunged closer. Finally, breath heavy, Teagan unwrapped the rotten rabbit leg and withdrew Cress's dagger. The noise of bone grinding against bone receded until they stopped completely. When she looked up from her pack, the bones had settled back in their places, no longer hungry for the human soul who'd trespassed upon their domain.

Cress had saved two legs from the rabbit she'd hunted days ago, and had left them to rot out in the sun, hung from the washing line in the backyard to keep it safe from foxes. The stench was horrible, but Teagan held the meat close to her chest, fearful that if she took her hand far enough away from her body, the bones would sense her human soul and wake again. Teagan paused to light a harmona leaf to try to calm herself and cover the stench. The commonly-used herb for spells emitted a faint smoke that drifted in lazy spirals toward the sky. She held the plant in her left hand as she clutched the leg and the dagger in her right, the putrid meat uncomfortably sponge-like. All was still and silent. She breathed with relief as she made her way down the stone path.

She couldn't believe she'd forgotten the only rule of the Bone Way. *Don't let them smell the life of you.* The dead were always starving, waiting for those fool enough to try to get past them without protection.

"Past the Bone Way, where the dead rest hungry," Teagan sang to herself. It was part of a Shadow Princess lullaby her mother sang to her when she was a child too imaginative and restless to sleep. It'd been the only thing that could calm her mind, settle her down. Now she laughed, throat thick with grief, at the thought of a little girl who took comfort in a song about death, and the mother who indulged it because she'd understood the darkness inside her. Teagan had always loved the stories, even the bad ones, but a favorite had been the one where the princess saved the love of her life. As she walked the Bone Way, she remembered her mother's story, hoping that even in this realm, it would quiet her anxious thoughts.

Once there was a girl born of starlight.

She was beloved, the daughter of a blacksmith and a powerful witch. She sat at her father's knee as he sharpened swords to fight the monsters who'd breached their home's borders. She walked the forest as her mother healed it time and time again, when the monsters were gone but had left destruction and blood in their wake.

One day, when she was a young girl, a prince rode into town, bringing with him his strongest fighters. He wanted weapons, he told her father, to help his people vanquish the beasts. He wanted a spell to keep him safe, he told her mother, so that he could lead his people into a bright future when the danger was eliminated. People said he was overconfident, and perhaps he was, for when he and his best warriors went into the woods, none returned.

The young girl waited for their arrival for three days. When no sign of them appeared, she took her most prized tools and the knowledge her mother had given her, and set out after the prince.

She found him surrounded by monsters, all alone and scared and hurt. She threw out her mother's spells as if she, too, were powerful. She slashed at their claws and throats as if she, too, knew how to wield a sharp weapon. And when the beasts kept coming, something rose within her. Bright starlight, covering the forest and the creatures and the dying prince. When the light cleared, she dropped to her knees in the muddy ground and curled her hands into fists. She was so drained she almost didn't hear the pained groan coming from her right.

The prince was awake, and the girl stumbled over to him, her feet slipping in pools of a murky, inky blackness slowly spreading along the forest floor. She ignored them, didn't care about what they meant, because all she had eyes for was the handsome young man who had given her the flower he'd picked fresh from her mother's garden. She pressed her hands to the large wound on his stomach, saw all the cuts and bruises along his beautiful face and arms, the slashes in his clothes.

All she could think about was keeping him alive and bringing him home. Soon the same strange light that had enveloped the monsters and turned them into puddles began to seep into the prince, from her. She started to worry, to pull away, but then she saw that it was healing him, sealing the cuts and smoothing the bruises, knotting his stomach back together more deftly than her mother could. She didn't understand it, and it seemed unimportant when the prince opened his eyes and smiled at her.

"You saved me," he said, and she'd never known anything so purely right as that moment when she leaned over and kissed him.

They returned to rejoicing and tear-filled gazes. Her skin retained a pale glow, a shine that made people kneel before her in reverence.

She was the child born of starlight, the one that had been prophesied to save the kingdom from the beasts that had haunted it for years upon years.

Her father gifted her the sword his father had passed down to him, patted her on the shoulder, and told her he knew raising her would be his proudest achievement in life. Her mother gifted her the spellbook of her ancestors, kissed her on the forehead, and told her she knew her daughter had been destined for great things.

And then they let her go, toward her bright future and the prince she'd saved with her starlight.

The Shadow Princess's story didn't end there, though this was where her mother would always stop when Teagan was younger. When she became a wild, growing teenager bursting with curiosity, she asked her mother if there were more tales about the princess. She'd looked at Teagan then, appraising her. She nodded slowly and said there were, but that they were not happy ones. Teagan hadn't cared about whether they were happy or not. She'd wanted to hear her mother's voice as she lay in her bed at night, with the window open and the forest's sounds filling the room.

Teagan's steps were soft and quiet, the dead just as quiet on either side of the path, but her mind was spinning.

She was here, in the Shadow Realm, in a place she'd never thought to be real. It was like nothing she'd ever imagined. She wondered what her mother would say if she could see her now.

Suddenly, a loud, piercing screech rang through the air, tearing Teagan from her thoughts. Teagan swallowed the scream caught in her throat as she looked up and saw a black shadow against the slate-gray sky. It was as if time slowed as the airborne creature, with a wingspan nearly the length of her entire home, let out another screech so loud that Teagan covered her ears. She'd read about these creatures in Cress's book. It was a vulture of the Shadow Realm called a virampi, with long, sharp teeth and blood-red eyes.

How had it found her? Cress's book said they were part of the Realm's menagerie of horrors but one which didn't attack unprovoked. But she hadn't provoked it, had she? She glanced around before her gaze was drawn to the smoke curling up into the sky from the harmona leaf. Oh, she was a fool! The virampi had zeroed in on her. She threw the leaf behind her to distract the virampi and began to run.

It screeched again, but Teagan ignored it, her heart racing, focusing only on the cadence of her feet on the stone path stretching ahead of her. She thought she could see a shape in the distance, something that looked like the Hallowed Arch. It was close—close enough for her to reach it and escape from the terrifying virampi. She grinned from the adrenalin, a grimace born from desperation mixed with tender hope. Then her boot caught on something and she went sprawling. Her knees hit the stone hard, and she gasped with pain as she skidded roughly to a stop. She tucked her chin in and shielded her face, but the impact still hurt. She lay on her stomach, breathing shakily, and forgot herself for a moment. Until the virampi flew low over her head and she curled into a ball. Made herself into as small a target as possible before the monstrous size of the predator.

It swooped toward the ground, freezing the blood in her veins—but it didn't come for her. Instead it sunk its teeth into the rabbit's leg, which lay six feet ahead, having been flung from Teagan's hands when she fell.

"No, no, no," Teagan moaned, starting toward the creature. But it was too late; the virampi had taken the rotten meat and with a couple of flaps from its impressive wings, disappeared on the horizon.

She knew she'd never catch up to it. She had to get out of the Bone Way or the skeletons would eat her alive. Not her skin and meat and blood, but her soul. They'd gobble up the light inside of her and keep her trapped in this place with them forever.

She'd never be free of the Shadow Realm. Never be with Cress again.

That thought drove fire into her, and she quickened her pace. She didn't look anywhere but straight ahead, she didn't want to get distracted, but she could *hear* the bones. Slow and clacking and moaning. It was awful, and even though she was running, the dead were waking faster and faster. They were moving onto the path even before she'd reached them, already stretching their pale fingers toward her. She could see the stone arch clearly now. It towered above the Bone Way, its shadows blending in with the grayness of the sky, and Teagan knew that if she made it past the arch, she'd be safe—or at least, safe from the skeletons. She remembered Cress telling her they couldn't cross the barrier, before Teagan had silenced her with a kiss.

Her breathing was hitched and dreadful, her heart clenching tight in her chest, but she couldn't stop. Not when she was so close, not when she could feel the bones nipping at her heels. Suddenly, her head was wrenched back in fiery pain. A bony hand had snagged her hair and it refused to let go. Teagan swung her dagger up and sliced its fingers off. Freed, she burst ahead with renewed speed. Finally, just there, the archway rose like a beacon of light and hope in this otherwise desolate and deadly place. Teagan pushed forward and dove toward its hallowed barrier.

The clacking grew quiet, and Teagan looked over her shoulder to find the dead lumbering back to their final resting places. They hadn't gotten their meal. They would sleep again until another unfortunate soul woke them. But it wouldn't be her.

The Bone Way was only the *first* part of the realm. More dangers awaited her, but Teagan steeled her shoulders, turned her back on the bones, and stepped through the new archway.

Chapter Three

The first thing Teagan noticed was that it was *hot*. The air was not just warm or mildly uncomfortable—it was a heat that pounded at her temples, and sweat instantly soaked her clothes. She opened her eyes and found she was in a desert.

There was nothing around but sand for leagues. There weren't even any *bones*. It was just an endless, endless expanse of brown, nearly red sand and a midnight-blue sky filled with stars. Teagan's mouth hung open as she stared at the brightness of them. There were constellations she didn't even have names for, and she was mesmerized by the sight. As she stood enchanted, a voice slipped into her head with a soft whisper.

"Teagan."

She whirled around. Was someone behind her? Had she already caught up to Cress? But there was no one there. The arch was gone, and in all directions, it was just Teagan and the hot air sticking to her skin. An emptiness that made her skin crawl.

It was such a sharp contrast to the Bone Way, but Teagan

thought she preferred the cold and the company of the dead to the way this new part of the realm clung to her. She shrugged off her cloak before it could suffocate her with its padded material.

Another path lay at her feet, brick instead of stone, a clear line that divided the sand and stretched as far as her eyes could see. But before she could take another step, her legs collapsed. The run through the Bone Way had stolen most of her breath, and now that the adrenalin had faded, exhaustion enveloped Teagan. She imagined the creature's poison swimming through her veins, weakening her bones and her heart. Maradin had said she didn't know what would happen to Teagan the longer the poison had time to cause havoc in her body. She'd never seen someone get bit. She'd used countless potions to help Teagan, and when none of them worked, Cress dragged Teagan all over Wystira looking for a cure. But the only cure was to make a deal with the Shadow Princess. It'd been *her* creature that got through the gate, *her* creature that went looking for food and found Teagan.

Teagan traced the fingers of her right hand over her left arm, where angry red marks burned livid on her pale skin. The indents the creature had left behind. She'd have a scar there forever, even if she managed to survive her journey through the realm and convince the Shadow Princess to help her.

Teagan drew in a deep breath; it was time to move on. As she got back to her feet, a hot wind kicked up sand in her face. With it came that voice again, the one that sounded so tantalizingly like her mother. Teagan's gaze was drawn to the midnight blue above, and the starry sky began to blur. The voice got louder, becoming more like her mother and less like a ghost. "Teagan, you're here."

"Mom," she sobbed. She was struck suddenly with overwhelming grief and anger, the toxic concoction that'd stripped Teagan of her dreams and desires for years, that'd made it impossible for her to get out of bed in the morning.

She'd only been sixteen when her mother passed away. Too young to become an orphan. Images played out in her mind, of what life could have been like if her only parent hadn't died—the woman who had taken her in when she was a baby, after her birth parents died of a plague that swept through Wystira. Her mother would have been there to wave her off when Teagan moved away to the Academy. She would have seen her fall in love, and get married. She would have been there when Teagan stumbled, bleeding, back into Lefora. Teagan was sure her mother would have known how to save her.

The brick disappeared beneath her feet, and she was back in her home. Her mother was tending to the hearth, sprinkling herbs into a giant pot above the fire. She was plump and small, lovely and warm, but also formidable. She'd faced down countless challenges as a midwife and healer. She'd stood up to the townsfolk who'd tried to cheat her even as they asked for her kindness. She'd been invited to Wystira's High Council, the court of witches who governed the country, after a particularly gruesome birth had ended happily for both mother and child, and they'd wanted to recognize her for it. But when she'd gotten there, they'd talked down to her and laughed at her clumsiness and poorness. She'd walked out on them after giving them an earful about their terrible manners and never looked back. Didn't even stop for the night, just hopped on the next train home.

Drisila was everything Teagan had always wanted to become, and she'd lost her years ago. She must be dreaming.

Her mother came over then, placing her palms on Teagan's cheeks. "My, you look a fright. Was the train ride exhausting? Come, sit. I've got your favorite soup on."

Teagan let herself be led to the table, and then inhaled deeply when a bowl was placed in front of her. The smell of thyme and cheesy potatoes was deliciously familiar. "How is school? I bet the academy has been working you hard."

"Yeah," Teagan said around a mouthful. "Especially the medical classes. There are so many parts that make up the human body, I have trouble remembering them all. Not to mention the anatomy class, which can be horrible."

Her mother looked at her quizzically. "What are you talking about? I thought you were taking aeronautical and engineering courses."

"No, I'm not."

"Why, of course you are!" Was she? She couldn't remember now; it was as if there was a fog in her mind, obscuring her thoughts. She could only see edges of her memories, not a full picture.

"That was your dream, Teagan, all these years," her mother continued. Yes, it had been, ever since she was a little girl and went to the science fair in town, where a friendly old man introduced her to the world of innovation. Clocks powered by sunlight and moonlight, a mechanical carriage that could fly, clothes that sewed themselves. They'd been magical and non-magical, created by people as old as a grandmother or as young as a small child who'd invented a way to detect malignant tumors before they grew. She'd been enchanted by it all, had kept the fair ticket in the wooden box in her room as a treasure. She'd started educating herself, because what she learned in school hadn't been enough, and filled her books with her own innovations. And every year when that science fair came back again, with new inventions and new geniuses opening doors for a young girl who dreamed the same as them, she had been just as enchanted as that first time.

Of course she wasn't taking medical classes. She didn't know where that thought had come from.

When dinner was finished and Teagan helped her mother clean the dishes, they leaned shoulder to shoulder, inhaling the scents of basil and rosemary and watching the moon peek out of the clouds past the kitchen window.

This life was so wonderful, a path she would've taken had it not been—had it not— Teagan shook her head, wondering why that thought wouldn't complete itself. Her mother didn't notice, so intent was she on catching the moonlight in a jar for future spells. For the first time, she properly studied her mother. The lines around her eyes that always crinkled into a smile, the full lips that opened with laughter more often than anger, the bright red of her hair spilling over her shoulders and down her back. The strands were graying now, but age couldn't diminish her beauty. Teagan loved this woman so much. Her heart gave a painful squeeze at the sight of her. She closed her eyes and tears leaked out of the corners of them. This wasn't real.

Teagan let loose a sob and put her head in her hands. She didn't want to leave the dream, but if she didn't, she'd be there forever. There was a reason they called this the Sky of Lost Dreams. Each of those stars was one of her own lost dreams, paths she hadn't chosen, conversations she hadn't had, and the realm knew exactly which ones would strike the deepest chord in her. The ones that would lead her off the brick road and into death. The stars were there to tempt her, to speak what was in her heart. If she listened to them, she'd be wandering an unchanging desert for as long as her soul survived.

That was *not* how she was going to die, no matter how much

it made her heart ache to hear her mother again. She'd raised Teagan to be cautious and caring, to have a healthy dose of fear, to be self-sufficient and to do what was right even if the cost was steep. Even if it was difficult.

It was so painful to let the dream go. She wished so badly that it was real. But it wasn't, and Cress was still out there.

Teagan opened her eyes to find her home had fallen away and the sandy desert claimed her once again. She startled when she realized her feet were sinking into sand, not brick. She hurried back to the path, still visible from where she'd woken up.

The brick shouldn't have been there, but the Shadow Realm defied the normal rules of Wystira. The princess had shaped this kingdom of the dead with her own hands, her own magical powers, had placed these dangers here to ward off visitors. To make it *hard*. Because those who made their way to her? They had to be the strongest, not just physically, but mentally. They had to be brave and true to themselves, and they had to be *desperate*.

Cress had been desperate. So desperate she'd ignored Teagan's wishes.

Their fight last night was seared in her mind, an almost welcome distraction from the draw of the stars.

Two Days Ago

Teagan and Cress were quiet as they walked home from Maradin's place. Maradin's words haunted the space between them. *I'm not sure how much more time you have.* It echoed in her mind, beating out a steady rhythm of *you will die soon.* Teagan felt like she was crawling in her own skin, and she didn't want to think about this. *She couldn't.*

"I need your help making a sleeping draught when we get home," she said, her voice sounding hollow even to herself.

Cress didn't seem surprised, and she nodded. "All right."

If Teagan could shut her mind down for a little while, if she could distance herself from this, she could force it from her consciousness. She could forget about it. And she needed to be able to do that so desperately she didn't even stop to take her shoes off at the door before she went to the kitchen and started pulling ingredients from the shelves.

"Teagan, slow down."

"I can't slow down, Cress. I don't have *time.*"

Cress didn't respond; she grabbed her spellbook from the table and opened it to the right page. Cress had told Teagan she'd first made this potion to help her sister sleep after the death of her beloved horse. Cress helped Teagan with it now. They measured the ingredients and put a pot on the fire. They crushed herbs and chopped flowers. They worked in what would have been comfortable silence before today; they'd always worked well together. But now Teagan felt like she couldn't breathe in this small space, felt that Cress was in the way. Twice she'd snapped, and twice Cress had snapped back. "If you don't want me here, you shouldn't have asked for my help!"

"No, I do want you here. You're the best at potions," Teagan grumbled.

"Then stop acting as if I'm a nuisance to you. Please." She spat out the last word.

Teagan apologized, but the anger wouldn't go away even as Cress stirred the draught and announced that it was done. Teagan watched with impatience as Cress poured it all into a cup, set it on a small plate so as not to burn her hands, and held it out to her. When Teagan's fingers curled around it, they brushed Cress's, but Cress pulled away quickly. Well, that was fine then. Teagan didn't want to stay awake in this day any longer.

As she walked down the hallway to their room, Teagan realized where her anger came from. The longer Cress spent on this foolish quest, the more Teagan grew frustrated and bitter.

Instead of spending her time with the woman she loved, the woman who was dying, Cress was reading texts and returning from inns at all hours of the morning, smelling of dust and old books. She'd crawl into bed and wrap her arms around Teagan and whisper that she was getting close. Close to the Shadow Princess and the cure. Close to saving her.

But they'd run out of time, hadn't they? And they hadn't found the princess.

Teagan downed the potion in one swallow to stop thinking about it and slid under the covers of their four-poster bed with the gossamer-like blush-pink canopy above. She didn't stir when Cress joined her late in the night.

* * *

The next morning, Teagan woke with a pounding headache, as if she'd tossed back one too many glasses of wine. Cress's side of the bed was empty and cold. After she'd made a stop in the washroom, she found Cress at her desk in the den, papers strewn all around her.

"I'm almost there, Teagan. I promise. There's just one little thing I need to make sure of before we set out for the Shadow Realm."

"Cress, just stop. Please."

Cress didn't look up from the old book she had open. "We're

so close I can taste it."

"Would you please look at me?" Cress finally pulled her gaze away from her research, expression more guarded than usual.

"I'm not even sure this is worth it," Teagan said.

"What are you talking about?"

"Going to the Shadow Princess. Everything about her suggests she's not going to give us what we want, so why should we risk it?"

"You're not serious." Cress's tone was cold.

"I'm dead serious." Cress didn't laugh, but Teagan hadn't exactly been being funny. This was life-or-death for her. "How do we know this is going to work?"

"Because she'll honor a deal."

"What if she doesn't? What if she doesn't even want to make a deal with us?"

Cress shook her head and went back to the book. "This is your only chance, Teagan, and I'm not going to lose it."

"And I don't want to lose you!" Teagan's outburst seemed to take Cress by surprise, but she didn't stop—couldn't stop. "If we go, and you get hurt or you die, what happens then?"

Cress finally rose from the desk chair and came to stand in front of Teagan. "Love, I have so much faith in us. We'll make it through the Shadow Realm and back home, and we'll both live long, long years."

"I don't want your death on my conscience," Teagan

whispered, letting her fear show itself fully.

"And what of my conscience? What of my life?" Cress stepped away and ran her hands through her hair. "Why do you get to make this decision as if you're the only one who'll have to live with it?"

"Because I am too scared to lose you!"

Cress opened her mouth, and then closed it. When she finally spoke, her voice broke. "Please don't ask me to let you go." It was as if all the fight went out of Cress as she sank onto the sofa, head in her hands. "Not after you saved me that day in the forest, Teagan. It should have been me."

"I'd do it again. I'd do anything for you."

"And I would do anything for *you*."

They were at an impasse, then. Teagan knew she was being stubborn, even more stubborn than Cress, but she couldn't imagine losing her, especially at the expense of saving Teagan's life. Maybe it wasn't exactly fair, given how they'd gotten to this point in the first place, given that she'd risked her life to save Cress from the monster. Teagan knew Cress was just trying to do the same for her. But Teagan didn't want to carry this kind of responsibility, this *burden*.

She couldn't bear the grief. Not again.

While it definitely wasn't fair to make Cress bear it after she was gone, Teagan knew she would be okay without her. Cress was resilient and so much stronger than Teagan was; she'd live on.

"This is my wish," Teagan said resolutely.

Cress looked away, her jaw clenched tight. She didn't say anything for several moments, and when she did, Teagan didn't feel any better. "I'm not sure I can respect it, I'm sorry. I need to go for a walk."

While Cress was gone, Teagan lay in bed with their cats curled up next to her and decided on a course of action. She'd go to the Shadow Realm on her own. That way, if she didn't make it, she wouldn't also have Cress's death on her hands. If this was to be her last chance, her last hope, she'd do it because she didn't want to leave Cress alone, the way her mother had left her. Teagan just had to put her faith and trust in Cress's inquisitive, brilliant mind. If she followed everything in Cress's notebook, she was sure she'd be fine.

Teagan wasn't going to be the reason Cress died too.

When Cress came back, the moon had risen in the sky and Teagan was already half-asleep. She heard the sounds of clothes dropping to the floor, felt the covers being pulled back and the bed shifting under the weight of another person. She didn't move or turn toward Cress, but Cress still snuggled in close, draping an arm around Teagan's body.

As Teagan's eyes drifted closed, she thought she felt something warm and wet hit the back of her neck and slide down her nightdress, but she was too sleepy to twist around.

Chapter Four

Teagan lost all sense of time in this unending landscape. The stars were still bright and her mother's voice still whispered, but she gritted her teeth and tried to forget about the dreams. Even the dust of crushed coranderis petals, usually a potent repellent to magic, wasn't enough to completely mask her mother's voice. Coranderis plants were hard to find, as past Wystirans had nearly driven them to extinction, intent on destroying the sole means of rendering their power useless. Many who followed the Goddess's teachings of balance and sacrifice, of only using magic for good, saved the flowers and replanted them. They were carefully cultivated now by the High Council, and only those with special licenses like Maradin were allowed to have them and use them as they saw fit.

Teagan was grateful for the clearheadedness the petals allowed her. To distract herself from the allure of the starry sky, she recited the different areas of the Shadow Realm.

Past the Bone Way,

Where the dead rest hungry;

Through the Sky of Lost Dreams,

Where souls wander forevermore;

Down the River of Sorrow,

Where water drowns the mind;

Up the Desolate Mountain,

Where monsters roam the halls;

To the Deathly Palace,

Where the Shadow Princess waits within.

But underneath the recitation were more whispers. *Teagan, world-renowned innovator, has created an invention so marvelous she's being awarded the Inventors' Guild Genius medal for it.* Echoes of applause rang in her ears. *Teagan has done it again! She's found a way to bind moonlight to power engines.* Other whispers sounded like Cress. *Come home, darling, I'm waiting for you.* She closed her eyes tightly, trying to ignore them.

She kept her head down as she walked, and she almost missed the shimmering mirage of a stone archway on the horizon. Teagan nearly wept with relief. She was almost out of water and her legs were aching, her feet sore, and her face burned in the heat. She'd prepared for the desert, but she'd underestimated how long it'd take to get out of here. She wondered if Cress had fared any better. How long had it taken her to get through the desert? *Had* she even gotten through it? What if Cress was wandering the sandy shores even now, laughing with a dream-Teagan and living her dream-life? She couldn't think of that—she had to keep going and hold onto the hope that Cress was safe, wherever she was.

A voice to her right drew her attention. It was more solid than the whispers had been. Teagan paused for a moment and listened. The voice was high and cheerful, like a person speaking to a close friend. Teagan took a deep breath to brace herself before she chanced a glance over her shoulder. Someone else was wandering in the hot sands, talking to themselves. Could it be Cress? Had Teagan already caught up with her? She ran to the figure, but before she'd taken more than a couple of steps, she truly took them in, without her need to see her wife safe clouding her senses. Their clothing was different. It wasn't Cress.

For a moment, she stopped, disappointment settling in her stomach. But Teagan knew what those dreams felt like, and she couldn't very well leave this stranger in them. Teagan shouted at them, "Hey! Don't listen to the dreams, they're not real!" but they didn't move or wake up.

Teagan knew it could mean trouble if she stepped off the path, if the stars got hold of her again. She'd only been able to survive so far because she hadn't been able to let go of the very real pain of losing her mother. But she hadn't been raised to turn away from someone in need, no matter how afraid for herself she might be. So Teagan stepped onto the sand and marched over to the person lost to the stars' dreams.

The closer she got to them, the more she could make them out. They were definitely not a mirage. They wore a threadbare light blue shirt and black trousers spattered with holes. They were facing away from her, and she placed her hand on their shoulder, hoping to draw them out of their reverie. "Don't listen to them, it's not real," she repeated. When they didn't turn, Teagan went around front.

She reeled back in shock. The skin of their face was sunken in so far that it looked skeletal. The parts of their body that were exposed to the heat, that weren't covered by tattered clothes, were shriveled and dry, and the eyes. Oh, the eyes! Teagan shuddered. They were wide open, but they'd been burned out long, long ago. This soul was already dead and gone, and Teagan could do nothing for them. She considered waking them; was it worth it? Would it make any difference, if she could? If she were in their shoes, she'd want to rest. She'd want peace. She'd want to be in the spirit realm with the Goddess.

According to Cress, magic couldn't be used in this place: the Shadow Princess wouldn't allow anyone to ease their journey in that way. But she could try to call this person's spirit home to the Goddess's realm; it was the least she could do. Teagan placed her hand a breadth away from the person's forehead. "Traveler, you've been away from home for far too long. Your Goddess is waiting for you. Go to her and be free of this place." As she said the words and moved her fingers down their face, their skin peeled and their bones crumbled. By the time she'd gotten to their toes, they were dust mixing with the gritty sand. It was a melancholic sight. She was hopeful they were with the Goddess now.

"I'm sorry I couldn't do more," she whispered. She felt sad about their death as she walked back to the brick road. They'd been so close to the end of the Sky. They'd almost made it.

She wouldn't let that be her. She sped toward the arch. It bore the same elegant calligraphy as the other arches, but she didn't stop to read it. She just wanted to be as far from this strange and alluring desert as possible.

She stepped through and stood in a silent forest. There was no birdcall, no cracking of twigs as animals rushed through, no rustling of leaves in the wind. A rotten smell hung in the air, and the trees looked sickly. Their leaves were wilting, their branches broken and trunks gnarled, a gray hue to them like they'd been poisoned. It was as if everything was dead in here. Teagan *hurt*, seeing it. She'd always been taught to respect nature, to give it the care and attention it deserved. To take care of plants and animals because they were all sacred to the Goddess. They all had their uses and importance. But this wasn't like anything she'd seen back in Wystira.

She grew a little homesick as she walked along the new dirt

path. Even dead, the forest felt familiar to her. It reminded her of Lefora and their little house on the edge of the wood. She put her cloak back on, as the air was cooler here than in the desert, thank the Goddess. Soon, the trees thinned and she could hear the rush of water. Her eyes widened as she came to a river. It wasn't silent or stagnant, like the forest; it was bubbling with excitement and life.

A small wooden boat was moored along the rocky shoreline. Teagan stopped for a moment, mouth drying out at the sight of the clear blue water of the river. She was so *thirsty*. But she knew this place; it was the River of Sorrow. If you drank from it, you'd never stop feeling sadness. Never stop crying. It was a task meant to break even the strongest of humans who wandered into the Shadow Realm. Teagan looked around, hoping to find some other source of water that wasn't part of the river, hoping to quench this thirst, but she knew it was futile. There had been no pools, no small creeks in the unnatural forest. The path led her right to the boat. Despite the thirst burning in her throat, she had no other choice but to continue.

Teagan wasn't a fan of boats after the time she and Cress almost smashed into the rocky cove outside Lefora. The usually calm sea had suddenly shifted, a storm took them by surprise, and they'd nearly crashed. Still, Teagan straightened her shoulders and walked toward the boat. At least she could sit for a bit. Rest her bones. Prepare for the next step on the journey to the Shadow Princess's Palace.

She untied the boat and jumped in, using the oar to push herself into the river's current. It was slower than she'd anticipated, but it carried her along so consistently that after a while she could set the oar down and let it pull her along on its own. She took out Cress's book to pass the time. She found the indexes where Cressidae had gone to the effort of noting every creature of the realm. There were the virampi with their sharp eyesight and even sharper sense of smell. They were night birds, and Teagan was worried. The sun was high in the sky now. Would they come out when it went down? They were mostly vultures; at least they only attacked if provoked.

There were also insects in this forest that would steal your soul's light if you weren't careful. Teagan looked at the illustration and shuddered; with those huge spikes on their backs, she could only imagine stealing her light wasn't the only thing they did. She was grateful her time in the forest had been brief. If she kept to the river, she'd be safe from them. They didn't like water.

Teagan's heart skipped a beat when she turned the next page. She almost put the book down, but she needed to face it again. It was the grisleck; a terrifying horned animal with long teeth that were perfect for crunching people.

She knew, because that was the creature that sank its fangs into her arm. In tiny, neat handwriting, Cress wrote: *Its venom is lethal.* Teagan wished they hadn't found that out in the way they had.

When emotions threatened to overwhelm her, she closed the book. The flow of the water was calming, but it just made her thirstier. She pulled her flask from her pack and cursed when she felt how little water was left. She drank the last of it, but it wasn't enough. A part of her desperately wanted to scoop up a handful of river water, but Cress had thrice underlined in her notes that one mustn't drink it.

She sighed and forced her gaze toward the horizon. A stretch of blue framed by the greenery of the forest on both sides, as far as she could see. She wondered where the river ended, and as she reached for the book again to find out, the boat hit an underwater rock. It tipped over perilously and threw her hard against the side. Stunned by the pain blooming across her ribs, Teagan could do nothing as the oar fell into the water and Cress's notes with it. She watched in horror as the book slipped beneath the now choppy waves. All of Cress's hard work, weeks of blood and sweat and tears, gone within an instant. But the oar was sinking fast too, and without it Teagan would be at the mercy of the river's whims. She flung her upper body over the edge of the boat and stretched as far as she could to reach. Her fingertips just grazed the edge of the oar as the boat bucked again and her head plunged into the icy river. She screamed, inhaling water, panicking for a moment before breaking the surface. She scrabbled for the railing of the boat to pull her upper body out of the water. She fell back into the boat, breathing heavily, the oar clutched tightly in her wet hands.

But it was too late. She'd drunk from the River of Sorrow.

Chapter Five

Despair filled her as she lay on her back in the boat, a sob caught in her throat. She could feel the crushing sadness pressing her down and knocking the breath right out of her lungs. She gasped as memories assailed her.

Teagan was in her workshop when a knock sounded on the front door. She set her tools aside and wiped her hands down her apron before she headed down the hall toward the door. She opened it. "Maradin, what a pleasant surprise!"

Maradin didn't smile, though. Her face was serious and intense. There was a queasy feeling in Teagan's stomach as she waited for the town healer to speak.

"Your mother collapsed outside Tora's house. I'm so sorry, Teagan. Her heart is giving out on her. There's nothing I can do." When Teagan didn't respond, Maradin's eyes and mouth softened. "She's resting at my place, if you'd like see her."

There was a rock in her throat, and words wouldn't come. She let Maradin lead her into town. Maradin's shop was shut, quiet, as Maradin led her to the back of the building where she lived. She'd never been in here before, and Teagan paused in the doorway to Maradin's guest room where her mother lay in an unfamiliar bed.

Her mother smiled at her, but Teagan couldn't move, couldn't speak. Teagan didn't like the look of her mother, frail and exhausted, trying to force cheerfulness. "Come here, my love."

Teagan let loose a sob and crawled into the bed. Her mother wrapped her arms around her and held her while Teagan tried to come to terms with the impossible.

The memories of her mother kept coming, forcing the grief back up as if no time had passed. Her birth parents had died when she was a child; she had been too young to grieve them. But Drisila was the reason Teagan was who she was, the most important person in her life. Teagan remembered getting ready for festival dances and her mother doing her hair for her; she remembered her mother coaxing her with a cup of tea and a story from her workshop after she'd spent too many hours trying to piece together an invention. Memories, both good and bad, flashed through her mind. The ones when she was a young woman with her mother walking alongside her in the forest, telling her to care for the creatures within so they would become her friend and care for her in return.

But not all of them had cared for her. A *creature* was the

reason she was in the Shadow Realm in the first place, and the memories of her mother disappeared, replaced with that day in the forest when she had chosen Cress's survival over her own.

Teagan had left Cress behind as she walked further into Asoria Forest. Cress wanted to collect more ingredients for spells, but Teagan only wanted to enjoy the feeling of nature surrounding her. The roar of the waterfall ahead, hidden by the trees, always made her feel at home. She smiled as she strolled through the last of the trees to get to the waterfall, brushing away a low-hanging branch, eager to face the familiar sight of the foamy waters rushing over the rocks. She stopped. A monstrous creature stood in front of the water, sniffing the air. It was massive, as big as the bears that roamed the northern forests of Wystira, and light gray fur covered every inch of it. It snorted and pawed at the ground, as if looking for food. She'd never seen anything like it. It had a horn in the middle of its head, and long, sharp teeth. Teagan began to back away, retreat into the forest, when her foot stepped on a twig. The snap echoed in the clearing. The creature turned to her and let loose a roar. It dug its claws into the ground, ready to give chase. Teagan's instincts took over, and she ran. She tore through the woods as fast as she could, but she could almost feel the hot breath of the monster at her back. She grabbed a low-hanging branch and began to climb up a tree. The creature tried to scramble up after her.

"Teagan! Where are you?" The animal paused and turned as Cress emerged from the trees.

"Cress!" Teagan shouted as the monster took off after her wife. Cress screamed, and Teagan scrambled back down the tree and found Cress trying to fend it off with a stick and her dagger.

Teagan had always had an affinity for creatures, and while this one looked like it wanted to eat them both, she couldn't stand there and do nothing. She had her ritual dagger, but she called out to it all the same, hoping she wouldn't have to use it. "Don't hurt her!"

The creature turned, and Teagan continued to talk to it in a soothing voice. Many animals only attacked when they felt threatened. If she could calm it down, it might leave them alone. For a moment, she thought she might have broken through its rage. Then, its eyes narrowed, and it sank into a crouch, ready to pounce. Teagan watched Cress lift her own dagger.

"No, Cress, don't!" Teagan yelled, but it was too late. It plunged into the creature's side. The creature ignored Cress's attack, and charged Teagan instead. Teagan lifted her weapon just in time. It sank underneath the monster's chin. The creature howled, enraged with pain, and bit into Teagan's arm, latching on tight. Teagan screamed in agony, the fangs tearing through her skin and muscles, grinding into her bones. It didn't let go until the life left its body.

"No, no, no, stop!" She clasped her hands to her head and screamed. She felt, again, the weight of killing a creature, even one from this dead kingdom. She hadn't wanted to, and she'd tried not to. But she'd sacrificed it for herself, and after she said prayers to the Goddess and lit a pyre for the body, she returned home to find out she'd been poisoned. She'd forced her sadness over Maradin's diagnosis down deep so she wouldn't have to think about it. The river wouldn't let her do that now.

Every week, Maradin cleaned the bite while Cress held Teagan's hand. It was a fiery kind of hurt, but it didn't seem to do much to improve the wound. It was still an angry red, still unhealed and infected. Maradin sighed after she finished and put away the medical paste she'd concocted. She re-wrapped Teagan's arm with more care than usual. When she looked up, Teagan saw tears in Maradin's eyes. "I'm not sure how much more time you have, love."

"We're so close to the Shadow Princess," Cress said, letting go of Teagan. Teagan wanted to grab her hand back, but she was numb.

"She's not the answer you're looking for."

"You don't know that," Cress snapped. "She's the only choice we have."

Teagan felt distant from the conversation as they argued, didn't want to let the truth of it sink in because it would overwhelm her. So she stuffed her despair and the dwindled hope and the pain

57

in a box in her mind and locked it.

Teagan was keening in the bottom of the boat, curled on her side. A weight pressed on her chest, a darkness that enveloped her heart and soul. The box sprung open, spilling everything she felt. Anger rose in its wake, grief that she should have so few years on this world while others got to live until they were old and gray and wrinkly. She'd survived her mother's death and fallen in love, only to die before her life truly began. She wasn't okay with it. She wasn't alright. She'd tried so hard to pretend so Cressidae would feel better. She'd tried so hard to push her truest feelings away so she wouldn't have to examine them because she knew if she did, they would overwhelm her to the point she'd never be able to breathe easy. But now she *screamed*. She screamed for herself, for Cress, for the person she could have been if only she'd gotten the chance to live longer. She knew she didn't have much time left. She didn't need Maradin to tell her that, though she had, just two days before she stepped into the realm. It was why Cress had forced the timeline up, had left without waiting for Teagan to come with her.

Teagan hadn't wanted Cress to die with her. She wished her wife had just listened to her so she wouldn't be here now feeling all of her pain.

When she finished screaming, she began to sob. Huge, gulping breaths. Salt tracks trailed down her cheeks and slipped into her heaving mouth. She hadn't let herself feel her diagnosis, truly *feel* the negative emotions because she'd wanted to be strong for Cress. For herself. But she couldn't pretend any longer. She didn't want to die. There was so much she wanted to do, so much she had to live for.

The River of Sorrow claimed her so surely that Teagan was unaware of the boat steadily moving along the water. She was lost to the sorrow.

But thinking about finding Cress, about being with the love of her life again, brought that awareness back. She needed to be out of the river's powerful grasp. Yet nothing could quell the sadness, and Teagan drew the words to her mind and mouth before she lost the nerve, and spat a spell. *Release me from your thrall, you wicked being.* The memories stopped suddenly, the darkness receding until it was only the pinprick it'd been before she'd tasted the water.

Then she felt a tug on her soul. She wasn't supposed to do magic in the realm; every little bit of it stole her light. The price you had to pay if you wanted to cheat, if you wanted this to be easy and simple. Cress had made sure to account for all the possibilities, had filled their packs with things to help in the event they would need them. She'd told Teagan that they couldn't be witches here. It would be a death sentence.

And Teagan had done it anyway, because she couldn't stand the weight of it all. No human could. They weren't meant to withstand so much sorrow and pain, and this realm tested that over and over again. Made a sparkling, clear river a temptation after the journey through the desert. Made humans look into themselves; all their desires and hopes and dreams. Just so that they would be crushed cruelly and irrevocably.

While she tried to clear her mind as best she could, she almost didn't see the opening in the shore ahead. A rocky hole that looked out of place when there'd been nothing but forest surrounding her for ages. Teagan quickly dove for the oar and pushed it into the water, steering toward the cave. It was the Desolate Mountain! If she kept going along the river, she'd fall to her death: the drop at the end was so sharp and sudden it couldn't be seen until it was too late. This was where she had to be, and she rowed as fast as possible toward the opening. She breathed with relief when she made it through the tunnel and kept rowing until her boat bumped up against a stone ledge. The river ended in this small cavern carved out of the mountain. Barely any light penetrated the darkness of the cave, so all Teagan could see was dark ground and jagged points of rock that hung from the ceiling.

Teagan grabbed her pack and climbed out of the boat. A couple of lit candles stood on a table against the wall to her right. The piece of furniture was out of place here, as if it belonged in someone's kitchen. Near the table a trickle of water flowed down the rock face into a well carved into the ground. When she peered at it more closely, she saw there was writing on the wall in the same old language inscribed on the arches. She was sure she remembered this from Cress's research. It was called the Well of Fulfillment, and it was *safe*. It was meant for the weary traveler who'd gotten this far, a reward for not dying. As if this was supposed to make up for the dangers of the Shadow Realm. As if the Shadow Princess wanted to give people hope, before she took it all away. The Shadow Princess was nothing if not mischievous.

Cress believed the Shadow Princess would honor a deal with them, but Teagan wasn't so sure. Still, it was her only hope, and she would die back in Wystira anyway.

Teagan's thirst roared back to life, and she drank greedily until she was sated. Afterward, she refilled her flask and dug into her pack for the food she'd brought; cheese wrapped in flat bread, veggies, and some fruit she'd picked from the tree in their yard. She was famished—she hadn't eaten much in the desert because she hadn't wanted to make herself thirstier. While she leaned against the table and chewed, she pondered over the doorway on the other side of the cavern.

This was the next path. The *last* path.

"The Shadow Princess's Descent Into Darkness"
Taken from the notebook of Cressidae of Tyras

The princess began to seek out dark magic a few years after she'd rid their world of monsters and saved her love. She told no one of her desires for more power, and spent most of her days by herself in the vast libraries looking for old and dangerous spells. The kind of spellwork that had been banned long ago.

The queen was so furious when she found out about it, she nearly burned the princess's bedchamber down. She would not tolerate this, not in the present or in the future. The queen gave her an ultimatum: give up her quest for forbidden magic, or release the prince from their vows. If she wanted one, she couldn't have the other.

Unwilling to give up either of them, the princess acquiesced to the queen and acted the dutiful daughter. But in secret, she *practiced*.

The princess had been born of the stars, and she'd been prophesied to save their world with her magic.

She was barely seventeen summers old when she carried that weight on her shoulders. She'd been so young, had lost the rest of her childhood to this prophecy. Maybe that was why she strayed onto the path of darkness.

When the queen died, the kingdom passed into the hands of her son. As the people mourned, the son struggled to follow in his mother's footsteps, and the princess retreated from public life. She no longer visited the markets to give food to the poor; she was absent when citizens brought their complaints to the king. When people caught a glimpse of her, they'd comment on her gaunt appearance in private. They'd wonder at her snappish tones and the way that she wouldn't allow anyone in her rooms, even the servants. They'd gossip about her needing separate rooms from her husband, and they'd say under their breaths that the princess hated him. When they were together, the two were cold and hardly touched; their smiles were sneers and their hearts had hardened. Gone was the young couple in love, the couple who'd ridden out of the forest together, safe and alive and whole, the couple who'd saved the kingdom.

But hadn't it all been the princess? It was she who saved him. She hated that she stood in the king's shadow. Hated that he was crowned with all the glory she wanted for herself. Her ambition and envy festered, pushing her ever further in her quest for power.

On a clear, bright morning, the warning bells rang

throughout the city. A tragedy had occurred—but it was not the return of the shadow monsters that some feared.

The princess had slit the king's throat while he was fast asleep and assumed control of the castle. The bells clanged loudly across the homes and shops, announcing the new rule. And in the wake of the sound, the people realized they'd been wrong about her. She hadn't only hated her husband; she'd hated all of them.

A rebellion was crushed before it could gain momentum. The princess gave her people a choice: bow to her or lose their heads. One by one, they knelt to her even with burning anger in their eyes.

The princess hadn't simply been prophesied to save their world, but also to be its destroyer. The people had chosen to ignore the latter part. The princess was brought up with kindness and hope and light in her, and she *had* saved them. How could she ever choose the dark? Choose herself over the fate of those she had been raised to love?

Unleashing the forbidden magic, she shattered reality. The Shadow Realm was created, where the princess could rule in eternity, protected from the passing of time in a world of her own creation.

The Shadow Princess had destroyed her kingdom. In the centuries that followed, countries like Wystira rose in its place. Some countries abhorred magic and condemned anyone who practiced it. If magic were forgotten, no one could repeat what the Shadow Princess had done. And while Wystira revered witches and magic, those who sought out dark magic were punished for it. The world had let her history become legend and tall tales and superstition. If no one believed her to be real, they would not attempt to follow in her footsteps.

No one spoke her real name ever again.

Chapter Six

There was no arch this time, just a dark tunnel that seemed keen to swallow her. Teagan didn't want to see where it led, knowing there would be a monster somewhere in its depths waiting for her. It was the guardian of the Desolate Mountain, the final obstacle between her and the Deathly Palace and the Princess—between her and Cress. The monster was a legendary fire-breather; if it was not satisfied with your food offering, it would burn you to ash. Cress had theorized it might be pacified with sweet foods, so Teagan carried fresh wikada berries from the orchards in the south of Wystira in her pack. It was the sweetest fruit available in all of Wystira. If Cress was right, it would allow her to pass. If not... Teagan didn't want to consider the possibility.

It'd taken Cress weeks to procure them because the smooth, juicy fruit only grew in the sunniest regions of Wystira. Teagan had asked why she'd gotten so many, and she'd said it was *just in case*. As if she'd known this was how it was all going to go down, that they'd be taking separate journeys into the realm because one of them was just more stubborn than the other. Cress knew herself and Teagan far too well.

Teagan finally forced herself to move on, to leave the River of Sorrow and the candlelit cavern behind her. Exhaustion weighed down her every limb, but she didn't want to linger. Her soul's light was thinning; she felt it, even more so after she'd used her magic. The mountain was cold, and Teagan was grateful she had her cloak. There was some light from torches set at intervals along the walls, but it was mostly dark. And rank. It smelled of wet fur and mud.

As she walked through the tunnels, the ground continually sloping upwards, she wished she had her wife's company. It'd been the two of them for so long. Cress had changed everything about Teagan's life. Her mother had told her love would do that, and Teagan said she wasn't looking for love, wasn't sure she *ever* would be. She thought she hadn't wanted it, that it wouldn't be worth giving up on her dreams of being a great inventor for someone else. A relationship would only be a distraction. But Cress wasn't a distraction, and she'd pushed Teagan to go after her heart's truest desires. She'd given Teagan the space to find out what she wanted in her life. Before the attack, Teagan had started the process into switching her focus at the Academy.

Teagan had received a response on whether they'd accept her in a new program just after she'd been bitten. She hadn't opened the letter; she'd placed it in the chest in her bedroom and hadn't looked at it again.

Cress hadn't crushed those dreams. *Dying* had crushed them.

Teagan stopped when she came to a fork in the road. Teagan looked at the left-hand path, and then the other, uncertain. She'd read something about this, but every time she tried to recall the specifics, she couldn't. There were symbols and letters on the rock wall; carvings she could barely make out. She remembered there was a symbol she was supposed to follow, but again, her memory was slippery. She took a deep breath and closed her eyes, tried to focus only on the paths. She thought she might get an instinct in her gut, telling her which tunnel to take.

She chose the left one, but when she turned the corner, she faced a smooth wall. A dead end. Undeterred, she doubled back and took the second path, but soon reached another fork. She tried the left again. She hadn't walked more than ten paces before her foot stepped on air. Teagan screamed as she tipped forward, perilously close to falling into the black hole in front of her. She spun quickly, painfully slamming into the wall at her side. She drew in a few deep breaths before she felt centered enough to peek over the ledge. The sight of the darkness descending into nothing was dizzying. Of course. The path through the mountain was filled with dangerous obstacles meant to kill her before she reached the palace, and it had almost succeeded.

Teagan once again retraced her steps and took the other path. Another fork, another wrong turn, and Teagan could feel panic rising within her. What if she never made it out of this place? What if she'd come so close and she'd ruined any chance she had at finding Cress? Teagan stopped at the next intersection and sat down with her back against the wall and her arms around her knees. She tried to even her breathing, tried to find a calmness within herself, but it was so hard when the air was thin and panic was clawing up her throat. She tried to focus on Cress, on their first meeting. It'd been so right with them from the beginning, and her memories of Cress brought happiness and contentment. Even their fight and Cress's reckless journey into the Shadow Realm hadn't dimmed her love for her. She held onto that feeling now, and let it warm her insides and cradle her with stillness. Her breathing slowed, the tightness in her chest loosened, and she stood on shaky legs.

Her instincts weren't taking her the right way, so she looked for clues in the carvings above the doorways instead. She recognized some of the images from Cress's drawings, the creatures that roamed the Shadow Realm, characters from the stories about the Princess she'd heard as a child. The virampi and grisleck in one corner, the beloved queen and the handsome prince in another, dozens of people whose names were forever lost. She thought she saw a small, stemmed fruit that looked like the wikada berry she had in her bag. Maybe Cress had been right in choosing the fruit; maybe it was specific to the Shadow Realm in a way they hadn't discovered in their research.

When she reached another intersection, this time with three different tunnels branching off of it, she chose the one with the berry on it. A little way in, she could hear clicking sounds, dozens of them all at different intervals. "Oh no, no, no," Teagan whispered, peering into the dark. In the small light cast by one of the wall's torches, she could see hundreds of dark green beetles with sharp pincers. Hundreds of small, carnivorous insects moving in the shadows. She imagined those hairy legs crawling up her skin and biting into her. Teagan stifled a scream when she realized they were feasting on a dead body, tearing the flesh right off of it. She turned and ran back the way she came. Scenting fresh prey, the little scurrying feet raced after her.

When she got back to the intersection, she dove into a different tunnel, hoping the shadowy interior would hide her. She flattened herself against the rough wall, ready to sprint if the beetles found her. The clicking reached a crescendo, and Teagan's muscles tensed. The beetles poured into the intersection and proceeded the way Teagan had come without any hesitation.

She stayed in that alcove long after the insects' clicking could no longer be heard, until her heart stopped racing. So that wasn't a wikada berry; she should have known. But she'd wanted it to be right *so badly*. Teagan hissed one of the curse words Cress had taught her and smacked her head softly against the rock in frustration. And as she glanced at the images carved above the tunnel she'd hid in, she noticed something she couldn't believe she'd missed this whole time.

Teagan reached her fingers up and traced the star. It wasn't just a star, though. A crescent moon was underneath it, and hidden in the space where the two overlapped was an *A*. This was the symbol of the Shadow Princess, the one they'd searched dusty old books for, the one that would lead her out of this horrible mountain. It was the first letter of the princess's long-forgotten name. She was sure of it.

As she walked on, Teagan let her thoughts wander toward the Shadow Princess and her story. Teagan didn't understand what it took to make someone descend into darkness and create this realm, to give up everything she was and everything she could have been, just to feel the pulse of the whole world at her fingertips. The Shadow Princess was a cautionary tale. She'd had it all; the prince, the kingdom, the magic. She'd been loved and admired and she could have ruled with a kind heart. But she hadn't; she had destroyed it from the inside out and she had laughed while doing so. She'd become the monster she'd defeated in the forest when she was a young woman.

The pieces she and Cress had collected about the princess's story couldn't give them the why of it. They weren't privy to the emotions behind the princess's decisions. No amount of dusty manuscripts and speculation could truly answer these questions.

But maybe when she completed this journey, when she met the princess, Teagan would be able to ask her.

If she ever got through this mountain.

What if she lost her way in this place again? She'd found the right image to follow—so she thought. She hadn't encountered any more obstacles; no black holes in the ground or creatures chasing her through the tunnels. Being alone like this, stuck deep inside this rocky terrain, made her feel hollow. Made her tremble with longing for companionship, any companionship. Humans weren't used to the oppressive dark like this; they weren't meant for it. That was probably the point.

There wasn't a clear path here, and she hated that. But it couldn't be *too* easy. The princess would make deals with only the bravest and strongest, the ones who passed all her tests and defied the Shadow Realm she'd created.

Teagan had spent so long in the tunnels that when she turned a corner and saw the arch, she almost couldn't believe it. There, blocking the last magical stone arch, was a monster. It was huge, almost as tall as the cavern ceiling, its spiky fur a midnight blue that appeared black in the little light from the torches on either side of it. Its nostrils were flared, and it had a long tail that curved around its body. It blew out a hot breath, and Teagan flinched, fearful of its fire. But it stayed there, unblinking and almost docile. When she moved forward, it bared sharp fangs and breathed another warm and sickeningly-sweet breath. She pulled the fruit from her bag and stepped toward it as fear beat a steady rhythm in her chest. She had to approach it slowly, let it sniff her so it would know she wasn't a threat. As she got closer, it prowled around on its paws. She watched its almost square face and the spiky fur that covered it from head to toe. It was a little like the bears that roamed the forests of Wystira, and she felt calmer when she stopped just in front of it and held her palm out.

It was simply a creature of the mountain, and it deserved her respect. As long as it didn't try to kill her.

The monster snorted out a breath and then opened its mouth, swallowing the fruit whole. She grimaced at the roughness of its tongue and her hand was slimy when she pulled it away. She wiped it off on her cloak and took a step back. Wikada berries were small— what if they were too small, and the monster wasn't satisfied? Teagan had nothing else to offer, and it didn't seem to be moving from the arch. Would she have to fight it? Then it sighed and moved, curling into a corner of the tunnel, satiated and sleepy, closing its eyes in contentment. Teagan almost shouted in relief, but she wisely didn't and ran through the arch before it could change its mind and decide that she had not offered enough.

In a moment, Teagan stood on a high cliff not unlike the one she'd started this journey on. But instead of the sea before her, it was a sight she'd never expected to see in the Shadow Realm.

PART TWO

Chapter Seven

Teagan couldn't believe her eyes. A vast, open valley lay below, but it was nothing like the rest of the realm. It was *beautiful*. Sun-drenched sky, so green and alive that Teagan blinked, sure she'd stepped back into Wystira somehow. This couldn't be the Shadow Realm. There was birdsong in the air and echoes of voices and laughter. Laughter meant *people*. She couldn't make them out in this distance, but she could see building upon building, pearly white and glowing in the afternoon light. It was a city, the structures clustered together like in Tyras, yet the style of the houses was unfamiliar. In the far distance, a tall spire pierced the clouds. A spire like that could only be attached to a grand castle. The Deathly Palace was somewhere beyond these homes, the end of her journey and the key to getting Cress back.

The path from the arch led to stairs chiseled into the mountainside. The steps were steep, and she had to focus to ward off dizziness and the thought of slipping and falling the long distance to the valley floor. The stone steps were grown over with moss and flowers, and Teagan wondered who had built them. What horrors could await her in this place, gorgeous beyond anything Teagan had ever seen? Its beauty became even more apparent when she finally reached the bottom of the mountain, sweaty and legs so exhausted that she had difficulty walking in a straight line. The path was marble, polished smooth and shiny, and it slithered through the forest and the streets. Shops and homes branched off, disappearing among the trees. People walked by and stared at her, curious and interested, but they didn't try to speak to her. They must not get visitors often. They didn't appear dead, though; they looked like *her*. Like they weren't trapped souls but merely people going about their daily life. They sauntered across bridges strung between trees, swam in the clear pool of the waterfall. They played music on the streets and danced freely in an open square. Vendors lined the area, but the people didn't haggle over prices. They simply traded goods and exchanged polite conversation. She was surprised she could understand most of it. It was not the old language on the arches or the Wystiran language. It was the language of the Shadow Realm.

After a while, the path grew so convoluted Teagan thought she'd lost it. The streets grew familiar; she could have sworn she'd seen that fountain once already. She started to reach for her pack before she remembered she didn't have the notebook. She groaned; there was probably an answer to her confusion, some way for her to tell the difference between the walkways. The dizziness that had left when she'd gotten down the mountain returned in full force.

Teagan walked over to an elderly woman sitting on a bench in front of the fountain. "Excuse me? Do you know where I might find the princess?" she asked, but the woman only smiled benignly at her and did not respond.

"Do you know the way to the palace?" she asked a young man selling artwork. He shook his head and brushed her aside for another patron.

She asked a few more people, but no one wanted anything to do with her. Perhaps the Princess didn't want them speaking to strangers.

Teagan walked down another street and found herself in a market. She turned in a circle, looking for a sign or another path, but the crush of bodies, so overwhelming after the solitude of her journey, was too much. Teagan bent at the waist, panic starting to sink in.

"Are you all right?"

She drew in a deep, gasping breath before she looked up to find a young girl in front of her. She had long brown hair, a heart-shaped face, and a gap between her front teeth. The girl smiled. "Most find this place disorienting."

"So how do you deal with it?"

"I was born here." She gestured around them. "This is my

home."

How was this possible? The research hadn't given them any indication that anyone lived with the Shadow Princess aside from those poor and unfortunate souls who got trapped here. How had they missed an entire city? People born in this place? Where were the stories about *them*? When Teagan straightened, she realized the girl was still waiting there, watching her with unguarded curiosity.

"We don't get a lot of travelers anymore," she said. "Where are you from?"

"Wystira," she replied, feeling homesick and heartsick without Cress.

"Oh! Just like that other lady!"

Teagan paused, completely and utterly shocked. "What other lady?"

"The one who came through here two days ago." As Teagan described her, the girl kept nodding after each detail, leaving Teagan with no doubt about it. Cress was here, and she was so close.

"Do you know where she is?"

The young girl hesitated. "With the queen."

"Can you take me there?"

"Mother says I'm not supposed to talk to the travelers or help them." She rolled her eyes, clearly unimpressed with her mother's rule. Teagan wondered if that was a rule of the Princess as well.

"Please, I must find my wife. She came here for me and I have to get her back."

The girl brightened. "A quest for love! My favorite!" She waved Teagan to follow her, and so she did, through back alleys and down quiet streets, past games being played by other children and people shopping. The girl told Teagan a story about a couple who'd journeyed to the realm because of their love for one another, back when the realm was quite new.

"It was a very long time ago, even older than grandmother and grandfather!" She skipped over the marble path, calling out to everyone she met. She was clearly adored, and was given many treats and pats on the head as they hurried along. "They were married just like you two, but the woman died on her wedding day. Her husband loved her so much that he followed her soul down to bargain for her release."

"What happened to them?"

The girl stopped short, but Teagan didn't realize it until she'd walked several paces ahead. She turned back around and was troubled by the expression on the girl's face. "The husband didn't follow Queen Amalaris's rules." *Amalaris.*

Teagan wanted to ask more about it, but the girl brightened. "But that was a long time ago!"

"Has anyone ever made it out?"

The girl's brows furrowed. "I don't think so." The girl

chattered on as if she hadn't just taken all of Teagan's last hopes and crushed them.

Before long they finally came upon the Deathly Palace. The building was impressive; with its huge spires it towered well over the valley. Its long columns bore images Teagan wished she had the time to examine closely. It was built out of the same pristine white stone as the rest of the city, and not even a speck of dirt clung to it. She thought of her house; all the mud tracked in from the woods, the cat hairs so entangled with the threads of the rugs that they'd never come out, the worn-in spots of the floorboards from all of Cress's pacing. She preferred the lived-in feel, despite all the opulence of the palace.

It made her feel like she was in a tomb.

"Thank you," Teagan told the girl.

"I hope you'll be able to get your wife back, like that one fellow!"

Teagan almost laughed with nerves; she didn't want to be like that unfortunate man. He hadn't gotten his wish. He and his wife hadn't made it home safe. Were they still in this realm, she wondered, lost in the desert or laid to rest on the Bone Way? Teagan shuddered, but the girl didn't notice and skipped off.

Steeling her resolve, Teagan pushed open the wide, double doors of the palace. No guards flanked them. The Shadow Princess did not need protection. She stepped into the palace. It was eerily quiet. No servants bustled about or greeted her; there weren't any flower arrangements in vases or paintings on the walls. It was just empty, solidly unmoving, and Teagan found it unnerving. She'd expected it to be as lively as the city. She had also expected the building to be as adorned as the grandest houses in Wystira; she had thought the princess would flaunt her wealth. But her steps echoed in the cavernous space and she came across no one as she walked on.

The further in she got, the less she wanted to find the princess, especially when she reached a hallway that stretched on for ages. In mirror-like glass cases, wisps floated. Teagan moved closer to view one of them, and the wisp whirled in its case. She gasped aloud as a shape emerged; smoky gray tendrils shifted, revealing a human face. She couldn't make out finer details, but it opened its mouth as if to scream in soundless desperation. Disturbed, she ran toward the doors at the end of this horrific hallway. She burst through them and found herself staring at the person she'd followed into this dead realm.

Chapter Eight

"Cress," Teagan breathed. She only had eyes for her wife. Cress was here. Cress was *alive*.

"Teagan." At the familiar sound of her voice, tears filled Teagan's eyes. Cress looked healthy enough. She stood with her arms crossed over her chest, defiant and daring. But Teagan saw the exhaustion in her wife's eyes, the weight of the Shadow Realm on her. Her eyes roved across her body, making sure that she was unharmed. She noticed a dimness to Cress, as if she could see Cress's soul losing its light. She seemed all right for now, but Teagan's anxiety would persist until they were both home safe.

Before she could take even a single step towards Cress, before they could say anything else, the woman on the marble throne spoke up.

"Hello, Teagan of Wystira. We've been waiting for you." The Shadow Princess had white hair that swept to the floor and pooled around her legs, and eyes the color of darkness. She crooked a finger, and Teagan walked forward cautiously.

"Cress was just telling me all about you."

"She was?" The Princess's piercing eyes regarded her lifelessly. No emotion showed on her statuesque face. Teagan found it just as disturbing as the empty palace.

"I was listening to the story of your love, how you met and when you married." The Princess smiled, but it didn't meet her eyes. She was stone, unchanged and unmoved. Teagan had hoped to appeal to her humanity, but did the Princess even have it anymore? She looked like a human, but she was not mortal. "The way you sacrificed yourself for her."

Teagan looked over at Cress, whose expression was carefully blank, and then back to the Princess. Cress had been here for the length of several days already, and Teagan didn't know what this meant, but it felt like the Princess was baiting her. "Yes, I'd do anything for her. And I've come to take her home."

"I'm afraid I can't let you do that. You see, if I just let you go, if I just give you what you want, then all my subjects would be unhappy with me." The Shadow Princess spread her arms wide, as if to encompass all her people in the valley.

She wouldn't let them go. After all Teagan and Cress had gone through, the Shadow Princess wouldn't let them leave the Shadow Realm. Teagan's thoughts raced, thinking of all the souls she'd stolen with false promises and unfair rules. All those who'd been torn apart by the skeletons, who had lost themselves in the desert or had been drowned in the river.

"How dare you," Cress spat, her familiar temper rising. At least the Shadow Realm hadn't broken her spirit. "You gave me your word."

The Princess laughed. "My dear, I'm the queen of this kingdom of the dead. I don't have to keep my word."

Cress glanced at Teagan, red high on her cheeks. She was angry, but not just angry; this was how she looked when she was about to do what she wanted regardless of the consequences. It was how she'd looked that night they fought and Cress left without waiting for Teagan to come with her.

"She promised to let me go if you came after me." Cress turned back to the princess. "You filthy *liar.*"

"Now, there's no need for names," the Princess said, a cruel smile on her lips. Cress cursed long and loud, throwing out every single bit of profanity she had learned at the knees of her sea-faring uncles. Teagan swallowed down her desperate laughter.

Cress was so strong. She'd do whatever it took to get what she wanted or desired—she would fight to the very end.

Teagan had hoped she would be as strong someday.

The Shadow Princess sat with her chin in her hands, gazing at Cress as if she was a particularly fascinating specimen. Emotion sparked behind her eyes now, and it made her seem more human. When Cress was finished, she simply asked, "Are you out of breath and getting ready for a second round, or have you tired of your useless shouting?" The way they spoke so familiarly to one another settled in Teagan's chest in the worst possible way.

But it was easy to force away the jealousy that used to show up more often, because Cress was fighting for *them*. She hadn't come all this way to lose Teagan, and Teagan hadn't come all this way to lose *her*.

"Don't you bargain with people?" Teagan asked. "Don't you make deals for those who make it through the Road of Silence?"

"Not anymore," she said softly, quietly, and Teagan wondered at the story behind her words. What could ruin the Princess's desire to reward those who were strong enough to survive? But she knew she'd never find out, and it burned inside her, this thirst to *know*. This must have been what Cress had felt like, all those weeks traveling and disappearing into libraries, searching for the Shadow Princess. Teagan hadn't understood it then.

"We came all this way because of your story," she began.

"And what stories do they tell about me?" The Princess turned her full gaze on her, and Teagan wanted to shy away from the dark depths. The Princess was centuries old, and even though her face remained unlined, her eyes betrayed how ancient and powerful she truly was. "Are they the good ones, about how I saved the world from terrible monsters and united a kingdom that had been lost under poor leadership and a curse that only *I* was able to lift?" She tilted her head, saw the truth in Teagan's eyes, and smiled. "But no, that wouldn't scare children into behaving properly, would it?"

"What about the stories about how you destroyed your kingdom?"

"I didn't destroy it," she said. "I brought it with me." Teagan felt the truth of that sink in, remembered the young girl who helped her find her way to the palace. These weren't people who traveled the Road of Silence but *her people*? Were they the ones who lived during her time, or were they later generations? She had so many questions; she chanced a glance at Cress, who didn't seem surprised at all. She must have already gone through this with the Princess.

Teagan ignored the implications of that revelation. "But you chose the darkness instead of light. You chose dark magic, the kind that harms and kills people, the kind that leaves rot in its wake." Although it might be a grave mistake to criticize the Princess, Teagan couldn't help herself. The dark, twisted magic, which corrupted everything it touched, was *wrong*. It went against everything Teagan believed in, against all the teachings of the Goddess.

The Princess didn't deny it. "I did."

"Why?"

"Because my prince, my dear husband, didn't want me to rule beside him." There was anger in her voice now, a rage undiminished by the passing of time which was finally given the space to breathe. It was as if Teagan was the only one who'd ever asked her this question. "He wanted me to be the jewel of his crown, not share it. I wanted to be the queen. I *deserved* to be queen. He was weak and helpless against my magic. He tried to fight, but I had always been stronger than him." Then she slanted them a cruel grin. "And he regretted his choices, in the end."

Despite the Princess's malice and recklessness, Teagan couldn't help but feel for her, ever so slightly. She couldn't imagine being married to someone who tried to suppress her, who didn't let her be herself. Cress had done the opposite; she'd pushed Teagan to go after her own dreams and put her own life on hold to save Teagan's.

She looked over at Cress, and the love they had for each other was mirrored in their eyes. Teagan couldn't imagine her life without her.

"His soul is still in this palace, trapped in glass," the Princess continued wistfully. Teagan felt nauseous when she remembered the glass cases in the halls, the human-like wisps inside them. The Princess smiled that cruel smile again. "And I will enjoy adding the two of yours to my collection."

Teagan's legs shook. This was her last chance—her last opportunity to make her case. "Shouldn't you at least hear us out?"

"I already have," the Princess said with a gesture at Cress.

"Your wife already told me why she is here."

"But you haven't heard *my* tale." She didn't think it would truly matter. The Princess didn't appear to want to change her mind, but Teagan wasn't going down without a fight. It wasn't as if she had anything to lose.

Teagan took a deep breath. "I lost my mother five years ago, and I thought I'd never feel alive again. I went to the Academy, thinking I'd follow in her footsteps and make her proud of me." She glanced at Cress, who smiled uncertainly. "And then I met Cressidae. She was exciting and intense, a brave person with an artist's heart. She made me realize that I shouldn't be living for my mother. I should be living for *me*." She returned her attention to the Princess, but couldn't read her expression. "But then one of *your* creatures escaped this realm and went after us. It poisoned me and forced us to spend our days trying to find a cure, trying to find *you*, and I'm so tired, Queen Amalaris. Slayer of Monsters. Conqueror of Kings. Don't you remember what it was like to go after what you desired? Don't you remember how thrilling it is to find that something and realize you'd be willing to do anything to keep it? Give me the chance to truly live, with the love of my life. *Please*." She hated to beg, but she'd come all this way, *they'd* come all this way, and this was Teagan's last option.

The Princess was silent for several long moments, and Teagan felt her hope extinguish, the last of the hope she didn't even know she had. She'd spent these days fighting bones and dreams, sorrow and monsters, and she'd thought it would be enough. She thought she'd been her bravest and strongest.

"All right," the Princess said suddenly, and Teagan startled at the intensity of it. "I'll let you go. I suppose two people so willing to die to get each other back should be rewarded. It's been so long since I've had the likes of the two of you in my palace, and I find I'm in a very generous mood." Teagan looked at Cress in wide-eyed happiness, until the Princess spoke again. "But on two conditions."

"Anything," Teagan breathed. She couldn't believe she and Cress were going home.

"A test. You have only three days left, Cressidae, before your soul is mine. You had best get out of here before your time runs out." Cress walked toward the door of the throne room, towards Teagan, towards their freedom. The Shadow Princess cocked her head and grinned at them. "You're sure you want to leave before you find out what the other condition is?"

"What is it?" Cress asked coldly, mouth pressed in a thin line.

"You may not touch one another while you're on the Road of Silence."

Teagan's expression creased with confusion, and then she quickly drew her hand away from Cress's with a hiss, as if she'd been burned. Their fingers had only been inches apart.

"Oh, is that all?" Cress threw over her shoulder. What was

Cress doing? They weren't safe yet. And they wouldn't be safe if Cress continued to respond to the Princess with such derision.

"We'll comply with your conditions," Teagan added softly. "We'll go now."

"But only if you give me a binding promise that you'll heal Teagan." Cress stared the Princess down, willing her to disagree.

The Shadow Princess inclined her head. "Very well. I give you my word, Cressidae and Teagan, that if you make it out of the Shadow Realm before the fourth morning, I will save Teagan and let you go."

"The both of us," Cress countered.

"The both of you," she agreed.

"Thank you," Teagan said. "For giving us this chance."

"Perhaps true partnership in marriage does exist. But don't forget," she called after them as they hurried to get out of there. "Three days, Cressidae. Or your soul is mine."

One Year Ago

Teagan sat in the armchair in the bedroom and sobbed. Her sheer, full-length dark red gown pooled on the floor and the cosmetics she'd put on her face would look terrible now, but she couldn't seem to stop. This was her wedding day, and she shouldn't be sad, but while Cress was in the den getting ready with her mother, Teagan didn't have hers. She was alone. She'd known this would happen ever since the day Cress asked her if she wanted to get married, and she thought she'd been prepared for the emotions to hit her, but they had still taken her by surprise. Even after all this time, the grief was there, hidden in the depths and rising to the surface at the most inconvenient of times.

The door opened a crack, and Teagan quickly wiped the tears away before she faced Maradin. Maradin took one glance at her and came into the room, shutting the door behind her.

"My mother wasn't around when I got married too."

Teagan's eyes grew wide with surprise. "You were married?"

Maradin laughed, the curls of her hair bouncing with the movement. "Yes, I was. To a wonderful man who passed away from the plague."

Oh. Teagan was sorry she'd never thought to ask. "I'm sorry."

Maradin waved that off. "It was a long time ago, and today is not about me."

Teagan sighed and curled her fingers into the soft fabric of her dress. "I just—I wish she were here."

"I know you do, and I know she would wish she was here as well." Maradin sat down on the bed, facing Teagan. "She'd always known this day would come, even when you swore up and down you'd never marry."

Teagan laughed remembering her stubbornness. "She always told me someone would sweep me off my feet if I wasn't careful. But I never had a chance when I met Cress. I was hers from the day we met." They had kissed right after Cress had finished painting Teagan and the night had grown dark with longing. They'd lain on that balcony until the sun rose, exploring each other's bodies in the coverage of the trees in the garden. Cress had whispered a spell to cocoon them from wandering eyes and keep them warm. Teagan had never felt so perfectly happy before that day.

When Cress asked Teagan to marry her, it felt right. A celebration of their love for one another. She *was* happy to spend the rest of her life with Cress, Goddess willing. But she missed her mom desperately.

Maradin must have sensed that, because she rose and surveyed the state of the cosmetics Teagan had so painstakingly applied before she'd washed them away with her tears. She could've said some kind of spell to fix it, but she'd been too lost in her sadness. Maradin did that now, passing a hand over Teagan's face as she spoke a few words under her breath. Maradin had practiced her craft for so long that she hardly needed to say the words aloud, unlike Teagan. Perhaps Maradin spoke the words to comfort her. "I'll have to reapply everything. I only got rid of all the marks of your crying."

Teagan felt herself blush a little at Maradin's matter-of-fact way of speaking, slightly ashamed of her ugly sobbing. But Maradin brushed over it as she swept Teagan's hair away from her face and fixed her makeup. It was soothing with Maradin here, acting the part of her mother, and Teagan blurted, "Would you walk me to Cress tonight?"

Maradin paused and Teagan thought she'd made a mistake, but when she looked up, she saw the shine of tears in Maradin's eyes. "I would be honored, Teagan." She cleared her throat and got back to work, and Teagan hid a smile. Maradin had always been unsure of herself when it came to displaying her emotions. In all the time she'd known her, Teagan had never seen her cry.

When she was finished, Maradin left to check if Cress was ready. The sun had set, and the full moon was high in the sky. For those who worshiped the Goddess, weddings almost always took place at night, when the moon could witness the joyous unions. For Teagan and Cress, the moon had been the first to witness their love, so it held a special place in their hearts.

Their wedding was held in the Asoria Forest. Maradin, with Teagan's arm looped through hers, led her along the path of orange and red petals between the trees. Wisps of light hung at intervals, illuminating their way. People stood in the grassy clearing, and the air hummed with their excitement. The breeze was cool and ruffled her skirts, and the moon shone down upon them. The arch at the center of the clearing was strung with flowers and leaves in fiery colors.

Cress stood in front of it, waiting for her. Cress's cream-colored gown was cinched in at the waist but the skirt was wide and flowing, and the dress dipped low between her breasts. Teagan's breath caught at the sight. She wore a crown of oak, strung with flowers, and a few more flowers were woven between Cress's curls. Teagan didn't have as many, but she did have her own crown made of the same oak as Cress's. Instead of flowers, animal figures were carved into it, cats and foxes, rabbits and bears.

As Maradin walked Teagan to Cress, Teagan didn't even see the family and friends gathered around them. All that mattered was her and Cress. Cress took Teagan's hands and brought them to her lips, giving them a soft kiss. She smiled widely, her eyes shining.

"Teagan of Lefora, the greatest pleasure you could have given me in life is choosing me as your wife. I promise to love and care for you, to be there when you need me and to get lost when you don't." The crowd chuckled, and Teagan rolled her eyes. "I promise to always challenge you and have your best interests at heart. In this, I am yours."

"Cressidae of Tyras, I always said I never wanted to get married, but then I met you." More chuckles sounded at that. "I promise to love and care for you, to keep you drowning in books and to be your muse for as long as you will have me. I promise to always keep you safe and follow you anywhere you want to go. In this, I am yours."

As they said their vows, a spark of light shot down from the moon, as if the Goddess herself had given them her blessing. They laughed in delight and kissed passionately. "I can't wait until we're alone," Teagan whispered in Cress's ear.

Cress leaned close and whispered, "Not yet, love." But when Cress kissed her again, Teagan could feel her hunger. It would be a long wait, but it would be worth it.

The arch was moved out of the clearing so everyone could dance. There were tables set up around the perimeter, and some held dishes of food and cake. Friends and family offered them well-wishes and blessings for a happy life together.

"May you always bring each other joy," Cress's mother said.

She was a thin, tall woman with severe features. She surprised Teagan with a hug. Cress's father stood beside her, a bear of a man with a quick smile. He twirled her around the clearing, her skirts billowing in the wind. Teagan stepped away only to be swept up by one of Cress's seafaring uncles, Mitas. Mitas's partner, a man with dark skin sharply dressed in a suit, told Teagan a story that brought tears to her eyes while they danced.

When Teagan thought she might faint with exhaustion, she excused herself to the refreshments table. As she gulped down a glass of water, Cress introduced her to a few of her childhood friends.

"I can't believe someone finally snagged the beauty of Tyras," said a woman with brown skin and curly brown hair. She smirked at Cress.

Cress rolled her eyes. "Please. *I'm* the lucky one." She gazed up at Teagan with a wide, open smile. "She's everything I could have wanted." Teagan beamed at her wife.

"We can see that," said a pale person with their hair arranged in a jumbled mess on their head. "We wish you both a lifetime of happiness." They gave Teagan a hug, and then pulled Cress into a fast dance. Cress's laughter trailed behind her, full and loud and bright. The night bloomed with love.

Cress had so many people surrounding her and they'd brought Teagan into the fold so easily and quickly. It warmed her heart, and she danced with a bliss she'd never felt before.

When people got tired and headed back to their homes or inns, the two of them retreated to their house.

"I have a surprise for you," Teagan said as they walked to their bedroom.

"It can wait," Cress replied, nipping at her ears.

Teagan giggled. "I promise it'll be worth it." Teagan went to the chest that held her most prized possessions and took out the wrapped gift.

Cress opened it fervently, and her face glowed when she lifted the pocket watch out.

"Teagan, it's beautiful."

Teagan had worked on it for weeks, taking apart old watches and putting the pieces she wanted back together. It was a deep red edged with gold, and displayed a clock face with the moon phases on it. Cress had lost her old timepiece in the forest, and she'd mourned its disappearance. It had held sentimental value to her. Teagan hoped this watch would make up for that. Cress smiled warmly. "I will treasure this forever, love."

Cress kissed her deeply, running her hands down Teagan's sides, and Teagan finally got to see Cress's dress on the floor of their bedroom.

Chapter Nine

Teagan shivered as they passed the hall with the Princess's soul collection. Hundreds upon hundreds of glass cases lined the hallway. The thought of ending up there, trapped forever, stopped her in her tracks.

When Cress realized she wasn't moving, she came back but stayed a little way off, that condition of the Princess on both of their minds. "We're not going to end up there."

"How can you be so sure?"

"Teagan, look at me." Teagan tore her gaze away from the souls. Cress's whole demeanor had softened, and there was a grin on her face. "We've both made it this far on our own. Together? We're unstoppable."

Teagan wished she could be as fearless, wished Cress's words made her feel warm inside instead of cool. They shouldn't have had to do this alone at all.

She remained quiet until they left the Palace. As they walked through the streets, the questions on her mind began to spill out.

"What, exactly, is this place?" The princess's explanation had only left Teagan with more questions.

Cress shook her head, placing a finger to her lips. "Not here, Teagan. We don't want to get distracted, and these people don't understand anything about their origins. We'll just confuse them." Cress moved through the city as if she'd been born there. Maybe in the two days she'd had with the Princess, it'd been enough for her to feel acclimated.

Cress always moved through the world like that. As they'd searched for the Princess's story, Cress had been able to find homes for them in the short time they were in a new place. She'd familiarized herself with each new town or city in a way Teagan had envied. Teagan had never wanted to live anywhere but Lefora, and she'd never grown used to being in Tyras for her studies. She'd wanted to become an inventor, but she'd never imagined it'd be anywhere but her little home at the edge of the Asoria Forest.

The walk through the city was mostly silent except for Cress pointing out which street they'd be going down next, and Teagan could feel the effects of their last fight still. And as they climbed the steep stairs back up the mountain, they were both too exhausted and focused to discuss the tension between them. There was an intensity to Cress, too, that suffocated Teagan.

By the time they got to the top, they were both breathing heavily and nearly leaning on each other. They snapped apart quickly, and Cress laughed without humor. "I hate that witch."

"Me too."

Almost as one, they turned back to the city. "This *was* the city the prince ruled from, before she killed him and claimed it for her own."

"I thought it was destroyed by her dark magic."

Cress snorted. "The histories were wrong, about a lot of things. She simply turned it into the Shadow Realm. She enclosed her people in with her as she created the Road of Silence and all its horrors, keeping the valley and the city as lush and beautiful as it'd been during the kingdom's best times. They're all trapped, forever unable to age or die or move on from this place. And they remember hardly a thing about their old lives. I tried to ask them about all of this, and they couldn't give me answers. Their minds have been wiped clean."

Teagan imagined *that* was a horrible fate, but there was a temptation in never aging or dying, in being able to spend centuries with your loved ones.

But if she and Cress didn't make it out, this wasn't their fate. A glass case in the Deathly Palace was.

As if she sensed it too, Cress held her palm out. "Tay, I need my book." Her use of the nickname she'd given Teagan was so achingly familiar it made her want to hug Cress. But she couldn't.

"I don't have it."

"What do you mean, you don't have it?"

"I lost it in the River of Sorrow." Cress swore and began to pace. Teagan wanted to reach out, to feel some kind of reassurance or comfort, but the Princess's rules bound her to keep her hands at her sides.

"How did that even happen?" The anger in her voice made Teagan keep her mouth closed. She wasn't going to be at the end of *this* Cress, the one who made the calls and dealt with things with cold efficiency and distance. It didn't matter, though, as Cress wasn't waiting around for an answer. She strode toward the edge of the mountainside and screamed.

When she was finished, she closed her eyes. "Can't wait to leave this cursed, rotten realm."

"Same," Teagan said with a sigh. Cress was here, and they were heading home, and they were going to be okay. Cress wouldn't become just another of the Shadow Princess's souls and Teagan would no longer have this poison running through her veins.

Cress came back to her and rolled up her sleeves, as if she was ready to get to work. As if she wasn't panicking about the lack of time, like Teagan was. "Okay, okay, I think I remember the way."

"We just have to follow the Shadow Princess's symbol."

"No, I'm taking the shortcut because we don't have time." She bit her lip and seemed to think something over, before she nodded. "I'm sure of it now."

"How sure?"

"Sure enough." Teagan wished she was as confident, but she followed Cress, of course. She'd always follow her, wherever she went and wherever she was, Teagan wanted to be at her side.

The walk along a monsterless path through the mountain was just as silent as the climb, for a time. They'd been partners for almost two years at this point, been married for half that. The silence didn't feel right. They'd always been able to talk to one another. What had changed to make it so that now she couldn't even read her wife's emotions?

"What happened to you, Cress?"

"I don't want to talk about it." They'd reached another intersection, and Cress was running her fingers along the images and words above the tunnels.

"We have to talk about it."

"Not right this very moment." She straightened and pointed to the left tunnel. "This way."

Frustration began to pound a steady beat in her heart. "Our cats are fine, by the way. If you were wondering."

Cress sighed, but Teagan couldn't see her expression because she was leading them. "Of course I was wondering. I love those bastards."

"Maradin should be seeing to them if..." She trailed off as a sudden, fiery pain spread through her chest. She leaned against the rocky wall and gasped, clutching her heart.

"Teagan, what's wrong?" For the first time since they had reunited, Cress's unflappable façade crumbled and her face creased in concern.

Teagan tried to answer when another bout of pain stole her breath. Cress started to reach for her, but Teagan jerked back. "The *rules*," she hissed through clenched teeth.

Cress paused, but Teagan could tell she wanted to come closer. Cress withdrew her hand and ran her fingers through her hair. "Tell me how to help you."

"I'm not sure." The pain was receding, but Teagan still felt the ache of it. She rubbed her chest, frowning. It was as if her heart had been burning from the inside. As a thought occurred, she unrolled her sleeve and unwrapped the bandage on her left arm. Teagan sucked in a ragged breath. The wound was so red now, so infected and raw, that it was almost turning black at the edges.

"Tay," Cress whispered, staring at the wound.

Teagan pulled away from the wall and straightened, covering her arm up again. "We should keep going."

"It's so much worse than before. How long has it been like this?"

"You don't have much time left, right? Besides, if you won't talk about your days alone with the Shadow Princess, I won't talk about this." So stubborn, but Teagan didn't care in that moment. She'd kept her anger in because it would have been too distracting, but now she let it slip, just a little.

Cress sent her a dark look. "That's not as important as this."

"Which way?" Teagan asked coolly. Cress eyed her as if she wanted to say more, but she only waved toward the right.

Under Cress's guidance, they proceeded through the mountain quicker than Teagan had on her own. They took a few short breaks to drink water and share some of the food they brought. Cress had enough water left from her own journey, which they could refill when they reached the cavern with the Well of Fulfillment. By the time they got there, both sore and exhausted, they nearly collapsed around the table. Teagan could hear the rush of the River of Sorrow just beyond.

"I think we have a few hours yet before the first day is over," Cress said.

"How do you even tell time here?"

Cress pulled out the pocket watch Teagan had given her on their wedding day. "It works here." Teagan was surprised it did, considering the Shadow Realm defied the normal rules. But it wasn't a magical watch, so perhaps that was why. Cress walked over to the boat, hands on hips. "There should be a different tunnel to take, but I can't see it."

"What do you mean?"

"You remember how the current swept you along the first time?" Teagan nodded. "Well, there should be another tunnel in here. Because of the magic, the river should be going back the way we've come, a full circle. Then we won't have to fight against

111

the current, but move with it, back to the forest."

"You memorized all of this?"

Cress glanced over, a small smile on her face. "I couldn't leave it to chance. I read that book end to end for weeks."

Together, they searched the cavern and the river. They found the narrow tunnel at the far side, almost hidden by the darkness. They both settled into the boat, facing each other. Cress steered them into the tunnel with their only oar, and the sun was eye-wateringly bright as they left the mountain and started down the river. It looked the same as it had the first time, though she knew it was different. Trees stood tall on either side, a little more full of life here, and she could hear the rush of the water so clearly.

They were quiet for a while, until the boat struck a hidden rock beneath the surface and nearly tipped to one side. Cress expertly righted the boat, and steered them clear of further hazards.

"That's how I lost your book. The boat almost turned over, and it slipped from my hands. I tried to grab for it, but I couldn't reach it."

"Did you fall in the river?"

"No," Teagan said. "But my head did."

Cress's eyes widened. "You swallowed the river's sorrow? And you still made it to the Deathly Palace?"

Teagan looked away, not wanting to see Cress's expression when she said this next part. "I had to use magic. And I don't want to hear it, okay?" She didn't want to hear about how she shouldn't have done that, how she should have fought the grief. It'd been difficult enough to lose her mother the first time; she couldn't go through it again.

Suddenly the oar was underneath her chin, dragging her gaze back to Cress. "I wasn't going to lecture you," she said softly. "I was just going to say that you were brave to fight the river's hold and come out of it whole." But she wasn't whole, not really. She had so many emotions bottled up inside she thought she was going to drown in them if she ever loosened her grip on them. The river had pulled all the sorrow out of her, for a time, but she'd pushed it back in so she wouldn't have to examine it. She just wanted to get out of this place. She wanted to play with her cats and snuggle with her wife. She wanted to walk through the forest outside her home for as long as she could. For whatever time she had left.

Her dreams were quiet, now, but they were *hers*.

Chapter Ten

Cress steered them like the sailor she'd become under her uncles' tutelage, while Teagan focused on the horizon and the path ahead. The ruminating didn't help, so when Cress told her that she should get some rest after checking her watch, she readily agreed. Her sleep was fitful and cold, her body shivering under a sky that wouldn't change color. The same brilliant sun arched above them.

"Does it never go down?" Teagan asked Cress.

"No, there aren't any normal sunsets, or sunrises."

Teagan groaned. It was beautiful, but she missed the night, the moon. It was hard to sleep, but her eyes finally drifted closed.

She woke to a distressed yell. She sat up quickly, ignoring how her head ached because of it, and turned toward Cress. Teagan gasped. Cress struggled on the bottom of the boat, a creature looming over her. It was a taesrin—a lanky creature about half the size of a human, covered in brown fur except for its bare, skeletal face. Teagan shouted Cress's name, and it turned to look at her and opened its mouth wider than any human could, displaying its long, sharp teeth perfect for devouring. Teagan scrambled but the taesrin didn't spare her a second glance. It bent back over Cress, its long sharp teeth snapping only inches from Cress. She groaned, her muscles shaking from the effort of keeping the creature from tearing her face off.

"Cress, hold on!" Teagan yelled as she dove for her pack. She quickly pulled Cress's dagger from inside and struck at the creature. It hissed in pain as she grazed the tough hide of its arm. But the fur acted as a shield, and the scratch only seemed to anger the taesrin. It turned on Teagan this time, and as she struggled to decide whether she could hurt it any further, Cress kicked out and knocked it toward the end of the boat. They both rushed it, and in its confusion it stumbled onto the rim of the boat, and they managed to kick it overboard. It cried out as it hit the water and disappeared. They stared at the water, ready in case it resurfaced, but the river remained undisturbed.

"Do they know how to swim?" Teagan asked, still gripping Cress's dagger as if it were a lifeline.

Cress shrugged as she leaned against the starboard side and clutched the rail. There was a scratch along the inside of her arm, but it wasn't deep. Otherwise, her wife was unharmed, but she still groaned as she straightened and swayed, unsteady in the rocking of the boat. Teagan reached out to help her, before she remembered the rules. Those cursed rules. Not being able to reassure them both with touch was torture.

Teagan was still shaking. "I thought they only ate the dead."

Cress gave her an odd smile. "They do. My soul's thinning, Teagan. That means death in this place."

"You must be closer to death than I am."

Cress didn't say anything for a moment, and then she laughed, loudly and freely. She kept laughing, and soon Teagan joined her because they were the same now, the two of them.

"Oh, the irony of me coming into this realm to save you, only for me to be the one in more danger of dying." That set off another peal of laughter. Everything about Teagan's wound, the Shadow Realm, their fight, just seemed absolutely preposterous for a moment.

After they brushed off the attack, Cress began to row again, whistling the tune of a lullaby. It nearly felt peaceful, just the two of them on this unnatural river, and it made Teagan think of home. Of days when the two of them would be out gardening, pulling weeds and snipping plants for teas and potions. Days spent snuggled on the sofa together as Teagan listened to Cress read to her, the cats curled up at their feet near the fire. Even the days when they were traveling, when they were cushioned in rooms at inns or staying with friends of Cress's family, when they could forget about finding a cure and just feel joy in being in new places. They'd had each other, and it'd always seemed as if they could tackle anything so long as they were together. It felt that way now, and it solidified something between them that warmed Teagan during the rest of the ride down the river.

"I hate this part of the realm the most."

Teagan looked over at Cress, confused. "Really? I'd think the river would be easiest for the girl who was brought up on the water."

Cress laughed. "Yes, it's not too bad, reminds me of my family and home. But I was always afraid of the monsters who live in that forest." Like the taesrin. They shuddered and caught each other's eyes. They were both remembering that day, back in Wystira, when they faced off against another of the Princess's creatures.

"Ever since we came upon the grisleck in Asoria, I haven't been able to stop thinking of it." It was a whispered confession, and Cress tore her gaze away to watch the horizon as she continued. "I haven't been able to sleep because of it, Teagan." The exhaustion in Cress's face spoke of more than the toll the Shadow Realm had taken on her, and Teagan wondered at how she hadn't seen it before today.

"You've been hiding nightmares from me?" In all the nights they'd slept snuggled tight together, Teagan had never noticed. She'd always been a deep sleeper. Her heart ached at the thought of her wife terrified in her dreams, waking with cold sweats and having no one to talk to.

Cress nodded, but she still didn't look at Teagan. "I've had nightmares every day since then."

"Why didn't you tell me?"

"Because I'm not the one dying!" Teagan decided not to point out that that was no longer true. "I didn't want to add to your stress."

"Cress, I don't want you to hide things from me. I want you to share your pain. It makes me feel less alone in this." Teagan moved a little closer and lowered her voice. "What happened to you in the Deathly Palace?"

Cress finally glanced at Teagan, as if needing Teagan to anchor her. "She showed me what my life would be like when you die. She showed me how bleak and hopeless my existence would be if I don't have you by my side." Her voice broke then, and Teagan wanted more than anything to be able to hold her. "I couldn't handle it, Teagan. I can't. And I know it's not fair to make myself the center of this, when you're the one wh—who..." She trailed off and shook her head, not wanting to say the words. She'd never shied from the truth before, had forced them to face it over and over again, every time they went to a different town, a different city, hoping to find enough information on the Princess. Teagan hadn't felt as if she'd had a chance to truly settle in with her own feelings because of it. "I love you so much. And the Shadow Princess used that against me, as often as she could. She'd used her magic to delve into my mind and show me the same nightmares I dream up every night. She forced me to live out my deepest fears."

Teagan was quiet for several moments, processing. "That's what the river did to me. Cut through to the deepest sorrows and made me *look* at them." Teagan glanced at her wife, tears in her eyes. "I don't want to die, Cress."

Cress let out a sound like a sob, but though her eyes were glassy, she refused to let the tears fall. It was the product of her upbringing—having a mother who forbade her to show emotions in public, of having parents who hid in mansions when faced with feelings they were uncomfortable with. Cress hated to cry because it made her uneasy, but she'd always known how to comfort Teagan. But the kind of comfort Teagan wanted she couldn't have. Touch had always been their most favored way of showing their affection for one another. With Cress's hand in hers, Teagan felt like she could take on the world. The Princess had taken that away. As if she'd known, and maybe she had; she'd been inside Cress's head.

"And I don't want you to die. I can't imagine my life without you," Cress said, her voice breaking.

"Is that why you fought me so hard?" Teagan asked. "Why you left me behind?"

Cress nodded, tears threatening to spill. "I couldn't lose you. I'm sorry I didn't wait for you to come with me, but I didn't feel as if I had a choice. All I wanted was to save you."

"And all I wanted was to not be a burden to you."

Cress shook her head wildly. "No, you're not a burden to me."

"But you've had to put your life on hold for me."

"That's because I wanted to, because *I love you*."

"And I love you," Teagan replied, and then steeled herself for something she'd needed to get off her chest for a long time. "Which is why I don't want you to let go of your dreams after I'm gone."

"You're not going anywhere," Cress said, as stubborn as ever.

It made Teagan laugh, before she got serious again. "We have to talk about this possibility."

"No." Cress held a hand up. "I'm refusing to participate in this conversation."

"You don't get to do that, not after you refused to listen to me and ran away to the Shadow Realm without thinking about how I would feel about it!" Teagan's voice rose. If they didn't talk about this now, they never would. Cress glared at Teagan, but it was without heat. "I know you don't want to do this, love. Do you think this is any easier for me? I don't like thinking about this. But I don't trust the Princess to keep her word."

"She will, if I have anything to say about it."

Teagan laughed again, but this time it was without humor, and it was wet because she was crying. Again. "I need you to listen to me. I don't want you to feel like you can't have a life without me. I want you to do whatever you desire, whatever excites you and keeps you awake at night because you can't stop thinking about it. Do that, for me, so that I know you'll be fine."

"Okay," Cress acquiesced. "But only because that's not going to happen." She stretched her hand out, letting her fingers rest just next to Teagan's. "We're going to get out of here, and you're going to live. I promise."

That was a hefty promise, but it warmed Teagan's bones and she felt lighter than she had in weeks. They were together again and they would be fine, whatever came their way.

But when they neared the shore to dock the boat and continue on the footpath, Cress's expression turned fearful. "More taesrin will be out now that we're leaving the water." She pulled Teagan's favorite ritual dagger from her pack, prepared to fight.

"I knew you'd stolen it."

Cress gave her a guilty look. "I wanted something of yours so that I wouldn't feel alone."

Teagan chuckled and held up Cress's dagger, and Cress burst into laughter. "I'd wanted something of yours too." They looked at the daggers, and then at one another, and smiled so brightly that Teagan knew it would've outshone the stars in the Sky of Lost Dreams.

After they jumped out and pulled the boat onto shore, they ran, their packs heavy on their shoulders. But after a few steps, Cress left the road. Teagan slid to a stop. "Cress, what are you doing?"

In response, Cress broke a branch off a deadened tree, the crack echoing in the unnaturally still forest. She threw it Teagan's way, and Teagan picked it up, the splintered end sharpened into a weapon. It'd be a far better one than their ritual daggers. Cress broke another one off for herself just as the sounds of wild animals rang through the silence.

"We've got to go!" Cress said. They tore down the forest's path as more taesrin howled. Teagan heard Cress cry out behind her, and she turned to defend her wife, but Cress managed to whack the taesrin that'd grabbed onto her. "I'm good, go!" she yelled.

The forest stretched on. Teagan could swear it hadn't been this big before. She wondered if the Princess was watching and had decided to lengthen the forest, to make it so they'd never get out. But as the thought occurred, Teagan could see the arch in the distance. She gave a shout.

Just as she'd come within six feet of it, she tripped over something on the ground. She skidded over the dirt and the branch flew out of her hands.

"Teagan!" Cress stood in front of her, using her branch like it was the mightiest sword, whipping it at the creatures with a fiery strength. "Get to the arch, I'll fight them off!"

Teagan ignored Cress's instructions, climbing to her feet and picking up her own branch again to join her. No way she would leave Cress behind like this. Soon enough, the four taesrin that had followed them were backing off, regrouping. Sensing their brief window of opportunity, Cress and Teagan dove for the archway and tumbled through to the other side of it.

One Week Ago

Teagan pulled her gloves on, the final touch to her outfit, and pursed her lips in the mirror when she saw the gown laid out on the bed for Cress. It was still sitting there, even though Cress had told her mother she would get ready an hour ago. They were visiting Cress's family at their estate in the southern part of Wystira. The harvest season was almost over, and that meant it was a time to celebrate, and to give thanks to the Goddess for another year of food and health. Cress's parents didn't really believe in the Goddess anymore, which was a spot of contention with Cress, but they knew it wouldn't be wise to abandon centuries-old traditions, so they hosted a ball for the harvest festival every year.

Teagan had been glad of the celebration because it'd given her a chance to get her mind off of her bleak future.

Earlier in the day, they'd had dinner with just the family, and Teagan had sent up a prayer to the Goddess for good health. The irony of it was not lost on her, but she hoped for a miracle all the same. She hoped the Goddess would spare her, but she knew deep down that wouldn't happen. Her wound wasn't the Goddess's doing—it was the Shadow Princess's.

Now the doors of the house had been flung open to receive revelers. Cress's mother had been bustling these last few weeks, putting the finishing touches to her ball, and Cress and Teagan had arrived in the middle of it. Cress had wanted to visit the library in the second biggest city in Wystira and continue her research. Teagan had practically begged her to say yes to the invitation so they could have a breather, so they could do something that wasn't tied to the Shadow Realm.

But the ball was about to start, and Cress wasn't showing any signs of attending it.

Teagan descended a flight of stairs and walked through a series of interconnected hallways until she reached the house's library. There was Cress, piles of books scattered across the massive oak desk, writing feverishly in her notebook. Teagan strode into the room, right up to the desk, and closed the book on Cress's hand.

"Ow, hey!" Teagan pulled it away from Cress. Cress tried to grab for it, but Teagan took a step back. "Really, this is childish."

"The party's about to begin."

Cress sat back and blew out a frustrated breath. "I have so much work to do yet."

"Cress, you promised."

"I'm so close to finding her, Teagan! Here, look at this." Her voice, excited and hopeful and bordering on all-consuming, struck a chord within Teagan. The only thing that mattered to Cress was the Shadow Princess. She'd known Cress had a particular fascination with her stories, had done a series of paintings about her and her past, but now it'd turned into a full-blown obsession. Cress thought of nothing else but that witch. "I found a diary from one of the priestesses in the old kingdom. It's the best firsthand account I've ever come across. Listen to this—"

"Cress, I don't want to hear about this anymore. I want to go to the ball and dance with you."

Cress's lips pressed together and she looked away. "We don't have much time left."

Teagan didn't need reminding. She felt the poison in her veins, that ever-present toxin seeping into every corner of her body. "Don't you think I know that? But we can spend a night away from it." Cress opened her mouth to argue further, but Teagan shut her down. "*I* want to spend a night away from it."

"I have to get through this book, but maybe I can join you before it ends."

"Cress."

"Teagan, I can't promise you, but I will try my hardest."

You already promised. But it wouldn't do any good to push; Cress had that stubborn expression on her face, and Teagan knew she wouldn't be able to crack it. Teagan threw the book on the desk, ignored Cress's muttered protest, and left the library.

Teagan danced with Cress's sister and brother, drank glass after glass of wine, and laughed heartily when Cress's uncles told her one of their stories. She'd almost forgotten her wife, sitting in the shadows of the library, until Cress appeared at the top of the stairs to the ballroom. People turned to gawk at her as she made her way down to them, looking ever so elegant in her silky forest-green gown, blond hair pinned back so it rested over one shoulder. She was radiant, and Teagan couldn't look away.

But she was still hurt that Cress hadn't come with her earlier. Teagan had wanted to walk into this room with Cress on her arm, to celebrate with her in front of all her family's friends and their peers. Now it just angered Teagan to see Cress blowing into this room undesirably late, like nothing was wrong. She'd wanted one night, just one, without having to think about death and the Shadow Princess. She'd wanted one night to have fun and get drunk and stay up too late, and then stumble into bed with her gorgeous wife.

Cress wove her way through the crowd until she reached Teagan's side. "May I have this dance?"

Though she considered ignoring the outstretched hand, Teagan did really want to dance with her. She let Cress lead her onto the center of the floor, and she sighed contentedly when Cress pulled her closer than was deemed appropriate and murmured in her ear. "You look splendid, my love."

"So do you," Teagan whispered back. Cress shivered as Teagan's breath ghosted across her face.

She lifted her eyes, soft and apologetic, to Teagan's. "I'm sorry."

"I'm still upset."

"I know, and you have every right to be. I promised you, but more than that, I didn't listen to your wishes. My time in the library tonight made me think about what we've been doing, our lives we've put on hold for this." Cress stopped dancing and cupped Teagan's face with her palms. "We shouldn't stop living because of this. We shouldn't stop being happy and joyful; we should be dancing as often as we can, when we can."

Teagan gave a long-suffering sigh. She never could stay mad at Cress. "That's all I've wanted."

Cress laughed, and then kissed her fully on the mouth. Teagan's lips parted as Cress's tongue swept inside, and her right hand came up to caress Cress's cheek. Her gloved arms were a nuisance, but she didn't want to stop kissing Cress to take them off. Everything else faded away until the only thing Teagan knew was the fiery warmth traveling through her body as their limbs entwined. Cress broke away at the loud clearing of a throat, grinned sheepishly at her older brother and his eye-roll, and then pulled Teagan out of the ballroom. Teagan's heart beat rapidly as they ran up the stairs. They stumbled into the door of their room, and then through it, tangling together as they tripped over a rug and went sprawling on the floor, lips never breaking apart.

They didn't even make it to the bed.

And after, when Teagan woke sleepily with Cress's fingers trailing over her shoulders, she couldn't imagine being anywhere else but in Cress's arms. Cress smiled and nudged Teagan.

"Goodnight."

Teagan laughed. She didn't need to look at the time to know it was very, very late.

"I'm too exhausted to get up," Teagan groaned. "I feel dead."

Teagan opened her eyes in time to see a pillow being smacked into her face. Cress glared at her, but it was without heat. "Don't say that or I'll set a taesrin on you."

"What's that?"

Cress grinned wickedly. "It's a furry creature with a horrifying howl from the Shadow Realm that only feeds on the dead. And sometimes, it gets out of the realm and can be found stealing people on death's door, particularly the children."

Teagan looked at her with wide eyes. "Don't tell me things like that so late!"

Cress beamed. "And sometimes they go after the healthy, just to keep things interesting."

Now it was Teagan's turn to smack Cress with the pillow.

Chapter Eleven

Cress almost fell on top of Teagan as they tumbled through the arch and rolled into the hot desert. They both let out groans as they rubbed their sore shins and elbows. Teagan had scraped her palm and she picked at the bits of sand as she wiped the blood away. She used the stick to help herself back to her feet. She should hold onto it—it would be useful when she became too tired to walk easily. Her mother's voice floated down to her, and she immediately put her hands over her ears, the stick slipping from her fingers.

"Do you have any more of the coranderis dust?" Cress asked, her voice sounding muffled through Teagan's palms. "I used all of mine." Fearing further intrusion from the voices, Teagan quickly withdrew the pouch from her pack and dumped some on Cress's open palms. Hopefully it would help protect them.

It was a grueling journey; she was grateful they had full flasks. She could almost feel her throat getting parched as she remembered just days ago, when she was wandering this desert on her own. And the whispers were back, louder this time, as if the Princess wanted to make it even more difficult for them to get beyond the next archway. If she was watching them, perhaps through the eyes of her creatures, Teagan wondered if she was pleased by their progress or scared of it. Although she'd given them this chance, she didn't think the Princess wanted them to survive. Or, if she did, she wanted to make them suffer as much as possible on the way.

The Shadow Princess hadn't always been like that. Even now, she had locked her own people inside this dangerous realm with her, but she hadn't let them die.

"I still don't understand why she did this," Teagan said as they kept their eyes on the brick road.

"The dark magic was so tempting, that's what she told me when I was with her. It wasn't simply what happened with the prince; she'd been practicing dark magic long before that. She'd wanted all that power for herself."

"Tell me the story where the Princess saved the lost boy who'd wandered too far in the enchanted forest," Teagan said, wanting Cress to keep talking over the hot whispers of the Shadow Realm.

Cress didn't respond right away, and Teagan thought she hadn't heard her or simply decided she didn't want to. Then, she started the familiar story.

"Long ago, after the princess saved her prince from

monsters, she became the hero of her kingdom. He brought her home with him and the people adored her. *Worshiped* her. She promised them that they'd never have to deal with those creatures again." Teagan let Cress's storytelling voice wash over her. The voice Teagan had fallen asleep to so many times over the years. The voice that would always feel exactly like home.

"But that forest where she'd fought those creatures was still alive, brimming with the echoes of hatred and hurt. It was still cursed. No one was to go inside; it was a punishable offense. Even the princess herself didn't step foot in it, for she wanted to set a good example. Yet she was also afraid, for though her power was great and her soul was immortal, it scared her. What she'd done that day had been terrifying, but she never let it show. And when a child wandered into the forest after the parents turned their backs for just a moment, she dove back into the trees without a care for herself." That definitely didn't sound like the woman Teagan had met back in the Deathly Palace.

"She used her magic to guide her to the boy, and when she found him, he was in the arms of a deadened oak. Its branches wrapped around him, as if it didn't want him to leave the forest. She said, *I've come to take him home. I'm sorry, but you can't have him.* She threw her starlight at the tree until it relented, giving the boy up. She carried him back to his waiting, desperate parents. And when she turned back, she thought she could see a glimmer of the once beautiful wood, before it'd been claimed by the darkness. By the monsters who'd fed and grown strong before she was born and became old enough to fight. It no longer scared her, and she was a hero once again. The shining savior of her kingdom." Cress trailed off, took a pause, before she ended it. "But she never did leave the forest behind. What'd called to those trees, what'd called those monsters to it before, it'd begun to call to her too. And one day, she listened to it. She let the temptation of dark magic rule her."

That story had always been one of Teagan's favorites even though it was the start of the Shadow Princess's dark descent. She'd been just a young woman who was fearful of what she didn't understand; a young woman who just wanted to do what was right. It helped, a bit, to humanize her. The Shadow Princess was a villain—but she had once been just like any other witch.

After walking through the tedious desert landscape for an interminable time, they took a break. Teagan and Cress sat near one another as the sky grew a little darker and Teagan told her about the soul she'd come across on her first journey through the desert.

"I'm proud of you for doing that," Cress said. Teagan had half expected her to lecture her about going off the path or using the rites because that could count as magic. It was a relief that she understood why Teagan had made this sacrifice to give the wandering soul the dignity of last rites. The dead deserved to rest easy, and the Goddess would have been dissatisfied if she'd left that soul alone, far away from the spirit realm.

Cress's watch ticked away their time steadily as they talked, but neither of them made a move to get up. It was almost day three, and Teagan was sure their time was going to come to an end soon. Because they didn't make it out of here before Cress's soul died or because *she* would die if the princess didn't keep to her word. So Teagan moved in closer, wishing she could rest her head on Cress's shoulder. Teagan was taller than her, tall enough that she could lay her cheek on Cress's luscious hair. She missed feeling Cress's arms around her; she missed being able to kiss her. A hatred towards the princess burned in her for taking this intimacy away from them.

"You know, I've been thinking about the night of the Harvest Ball."

Cress turned to her, a sly glint her eye. "Oh?" The heat in her gaze warmed Teagan down to her very soul; her fingers itched to caress and cradle Cress in her arms.

"That was a good night, love," Cress murmured. Teagan knew these reminisces were dangerous right now with that look in Cress's eyes; it was so hard to ignore the sparks between them. Teagan hoped they would never dim.

"What do your lost dreams sound like?" Teagan wondered aloud.

Cress cocked her head and the slant of her face took Teagan's breath away, had always taken Teagan's breath away ever since the first time they met. Back in Tyras, she'd wondered how someone like Cress could fall for her, wondered why she wanted *anything* to do with her. She still wondered that, sometimes. Cress shrugged, bringing her back to the present moment. "I haven't paid much attention to them."

"But what if they were your truest dreams in life?"

"This sky can't know everything that's in my heart, Teagan. It can't know what I truly want."

"The *Princess* knows."

"She knows *nothing*," Cress spat angrily. "She thinks she understands humans after so many years, but what she doesn't get is that we're all different. She can't look at one of us and decide that she knows what we desire. She doesn't know who you are any more than she knows who I am. And she doesn't know what love is. You hear that, Princess?" She stood and yelled that last bit at the sky, raging at the Princess who'd surely hear her words. Teagan almost moved to stop her, but she understood the anger. Because underneath it was the very same pain that'd brought both of them to this realm in the first place.

Cress continued her tirade. "Wystira's own Goddess, a young woman like yourself, fought back the darkness you brought into all the world and saved us from *you*. She's kept us safe all these years, and she's the only reason you can't spread your magic like a poison. You're shallow and deceitful and you gave it all up, for what? Death is your companion, always and forever. Those people in your city! They're only staying with you because they have nowhere else to go, because *you* took it all away from them! How does that make you feel, Amalaris, to know that all you've left this world is despair!" Cress was breathing heavily, and she kicked at the sand that'd spilled onto the brick path. In her anger, she stubbed her toe. She cursed.

"Are you okay?" Teagan asked after a moment. It was always best to let Cress get out everything she needed to.

"I'm fine," she bit out. "It's not going to kill me." Cress sat back down heavily, rubbing her foot.

"The sky showed me my mother, alive," Teagan said after a while. "It showed me doing what I've always dreamed of doing."

Cress softened. "Oh Teagan."

"And it makes me so mad that I won't get either of those things." Teagan pressed a fist to her chest, felt the poison running through her veins. Even when she was sitting and resting, it still clouded her breathing and made her feel tired and achy. "It's not fair."

"No, it's not. And I'm angry about it too. So, so angry I can hardly breathe sometimes." And Teagan understood that now, better than she had these last few weeks. The Shadow Realm might have been doing all it could to kill them, but it'd also brought the two of them closer together, forced them to confront their feelings and share them with each other.

All they'd done since they met, all they'd done since they fell in love, was put each other before themselves. Teagan understood, finally, that Cress left not because she didn't believe in Teagan or because she'd wanted to ignore her wishes, but because she'd been so desperate not to lose her. And wasn't that how Teagan had felt, when she'd found Cress gone from their bed and when she'd fought so hard to follow her? They should always have done this *together*.

"We should keep going, love," Cress said.

"How much time do we have left?"

Cress looked at her watch, and then at Teagan with wide eyes. "We have one day."

One day left. They quickly packed their things and got back up.

On the last stretch of desert, Teagan fell to her knees as a bolt of fiery pain swept through her chest. The stick clattered to the ground beside her, echoing in the silence.

Cress dropped down quickly and started to reach out, when Teagan gasped, "The rules."

"I don't care about the rules!"

"We have no choice, Cress. If we don't follow them, we're both dead." *I'm dead anyway*, she thought. She was running out of time. The best thing she could do was make sure Cress lived. And that meant moving again.

But Teagan couldn't seem to make her legs work, and the pain intensified, expanding into her ribs and around to her back.

Her mouth opened in a silent scream; even her voice failed her.

"Teagan, I don't know how to help you." Cress's voice was shaky and uneven.

Teagan closed her eyes and tears leaked out of their corners. She curled onto her side in pain. She felt something else in their presence. Was it a lost dream? As her body got weaker and her soul grew thinner, she heard the call of death, of the Shadow Princess reaching for her through the encroaching darkness. She had been watching them; she'd been waiting for this moment. As if she sensed this too, Cress shouted, "No, you can't have her! Goddess, help us." But their Goddess couldn't reach this realm.

A light rushed through her body, tearing through the agony that had overtaken her. She slowly regained consciousness, and when she managed to open her eyes, Cress was above her, eyes closed and muttering under her breath. She appeared so pale, so much paler than Teagan, as if she was dissolving. The full force of what Cress had done hit her, and she tried to sit up but her limbs felt so heavy.

"Cress. Stop." Cress continued her spell, though; she was so lost in the magic. "Cressidae!" Cress opened her eyes and gasped, and then she collapsed. She struck the stone with a sickly sound.

"Cress!" She wanted to gather her in her arms, but that rule. It was all they had left. "Please, Cress, wake up." Tears streaked her face, until darkness claimed her again. Her last thought echoed through her mind. *Please Goddess, do not let me lose her as well.*

Chapter Twelve

Teagan didn't realize she'd passed out until she heard Cress's voice. Her very much *alive* voice. Cress was stirring, and Teagan sat up with a jolt. She watched as Cress looked around them, slightly disoriented, as if she couldn't remember what had happened. "Teagan?" Her tone was shaky and hoarse.

"We're both still here."

Cress rubbed at her eyes, trying to clear the sleep from them. "How long was I out?"

"I'm not sure."

Cress took the watch out and gasped. "Oh no. No, no, no. There's so little time left."

Cress's efforts had been futile. Both their deaths reaching for them. All of her dreams had fallen to pieces in the wake of the lost time. They weren't going to make it.

"You shouldn't have done that," Teagan said. If Cress hadn't used her magic, she might have been able to escape. Now they would perish together.

Cress threw Teagan a sharp glance. "I'm not going to apologize for keeping you alive."

"At what cost?"

"I'm fine."

"Cressidae, you used magic on me!"

"I said I'm fine!" She got to her feet and scanned the horizon as if the arch to the Bone Way would appear if she just searched hard enough. "We've got to get going."

"What's the point? We're not going to get back in time anyway!"

"I will not hear that, Tay. I will not lose hope, not when we're so close." But they weren't close, not really. The arch could be anywhere.

Teagan didn't move. "It's hopeless, Cress."

"It's not hopeless until we're out of time. Come on, Teagan, what is that beautiful mind of yours thinking right now? Tell me you've got a plan brewing in there. Something that can help us." Cress knelt in front of her. "You're a brilliant inventor, love. You can come up with something, I know you can."

It felt impossible to force away the thoughts of failure, so difficult to hold onto the bright hope shining in Cress's eyes. "You need to snap out of this, Teagan."

She was trying, but it was as if she'd swallowed some of the

River of Sorrow again. Yet, hadn't she been able to move on after her mother's death? Hadn't she been able to make plans for herself? Hadn't she come alive again? She could do this. Cress was with her, and they loved each other, and that love was enough. It had *always* been enough.

Teagan pushed all of the despair away until all she saw in her mind's eye was the problem at hand. And the solution came so clearly and so simply she didn't know how she'd never thought of it before. "I need my rope. And give me the rest of the rotten rabbit meat you have." Cress's journey through the Bone Way had gone much more smoothly than Teagan's, and she still had some meat.

Cress's expression creased in confusion. "What do you need those for?"

"We're going to catch a virampi," Teagan said excitedly, as she searched in her pack for a harmona leaf.

"You're not serious."

"I'm actually dead serious."

"They're monsters!"

Teagan shook her head. "They're simply creatures of the realm, Cress. And creatures I can handle."

"Teagan, this is madness."

"It's the only way. We bring one to us, capture it with the rope, and ride it out of here."

"Madness," Cress muttered.

"The only way," Teagan repeated. Cress still looked wary and scared as Teagan lit the plant and set it on the ground, left the meat beside it as the smoke curled into the sky. With a sigh, Cress drew Teagan's dagger as a precaution.

The rotten stench permeated the air for a moment before the harmona covered it.

They looked at the items, and then at one another, and smiled tentatively.

All they had to do was wait. It didn't take long for a virampi to appear on the horizon, screeching in anticipation of a meal. It began to swing low toward them. Cress scrambled backward before Teagan could stop her, but the virampi only had eyes for the meat. It was hungry, and that was all they needed. When it landed before them, its large wings beat the air and stirred sand into their faces.

At Teagan's signal, they attempted to loop the rope around the creature. It reared up and screamed, and Cress backed away. In her haste, she pulled the rope from Teagan's hands. Teagan stumbled as the virampi swung its gaze toward her. It prowled a little closer, and Teagan, letting her fear override her logic for a moment, was sure it was going to kill her.

Taking a deep breath to center herself, she properly looked at it, this vulture of the Shadow Realm, and saw in its eyes not anger or hunger, but fear. *It* was scared of *her*. It stopped just short of her when she didn't move, but Teagan reached out her hand and stepped forward anyway.

"Teagan, what are you doing?!" Cress whisper-yelled behind her.

It wouldn't harm her, she was sure of it now. She didn't sense any malice from it, any intent to hurt them. When she got close enough, she placed a hand on its cheek. The virampi's skin was surprisingly warm. It sighed in contentment. Teagan let her palm trail over its sleek back and smooth head, and the virampi turned its nose so it could sniff her and nuzzle at her hand. Teagan laughed softly, delighted. It was just an animal, after all.

"Teagan," Cress breathed with awe. The virampi sensed Cress's approach, but it didn't rear back in fear.

"I was wondering," Teagan said as she gently rubbed its face, "if you'd let us ride on your back and take us to the Bone Way."

It snorted and began to stretch its wings, and for a moment Teagan wondered whether it hadn't understood or that it refused, but then it settled low on the ground. Teagan grabbed her pack from where she'd left it, and she climbed onto the virampi's back. She settled in the dip of its back and held onto the leathery fur covering its skin. It felt strange under her fingers, but it stopped her from sliding off when the virampi's wings blew a huge gust of wind.

Cress hopped on behind her just as the creature took to the sky and she grabbed onto Teagan with a loud *whoa*!

Teagan sang softly to it as it flew above the desert, one of her favorite tunes from a musician of Tyras. Cress sang along with her, their voices blending in a lovely harmony. It carried them through the day as the virampi soared under the stars and past the stone arch that marked the boundary between the Sky and the Bone Way. They could tell the difference immediately; the sky had turned back into that dark slate. But the virampi knew the way, and it flew low so that when she leaned over the edge, she could see the bones on either side of them. The skeletons hadn't woken yet, but Teagan knew it was only a matter of time. They'd smell them soon, smell that they were very much alive and well.

Or, as alive as they could be at this point.

"We have to get off!" Cress shouted in her ear.

"We'll wait until we're closer!" There, in the distance, she could see the stone arch. The one that would lead them to Wystira. They were nearly home!

Teagan held the walking stick tight in her hands. They counted down from three, and then slid off the virampi's back as it dropped even lower. They fell to the stone path, but it was a short drop, and an additional bruise or two didn't feel important when they were so *close*. They rose to their feet, rubbing at sore spots, until the clacking of bones stopped them cold.

They ran. As skeletons stumbled onto the path, they swung their sticks with abandon, and Teagan was grateful they'd held onto them after getting through the forest. She almost felt bad about hitting the skeletons, when she hadn't before, because now she understood the Road of Silence. Now she knew how hard it was to survive this place. But she wanted to *live*. She wanted Cress to live, and they were nearly there.

They were back-to-back as they forced their way toward the arch. Toward *home*.

A gust of wind and a sharp voice pierced the air and stopped everyone in their tracks, including the bones. The Princess materialized directly in front of the arch in a swirl of anger and fierceness. Her hair was braided and pinned up, her blood-red cloak swirling around her as she stalked toward them.

"You have disobeyed my rules, travelers." Teagan had let herself believe they'd make it, that they'd get to the arch in time. But she'd known, deep down, this woman would never let them go.

Teagan was so angry she burned. It might have been the poison, she couldn't tell, and she drew herself up to her full height as she faced the Shadow Princess down. Before she could say anything, Cress stepped forward, bold and mighty in the face of death. "No, we didn't."

"You were not supposed to touch each other, not a single point of skin-on-skin contact, and you failed." The Princess smiled. "I look forward to keeping your souls for the rest of eternity."

"No!" Cress threw herself toward the witch, Teagan's dagger

out and at the ready. The Princess pushed her away as if she were nothing, as if she weighed nothing. Cress tumbled into two frozen skeletons. They all crashed in a jumbled mess, but she was up and ready to fight again before Teagan could reach her.

"You're not playing fair, Amalaris." Cress said, holding the dagger as if it would do anything to stop someone so powerful. "We made it here on time."

"Do not worry, Cressidae, I will savor our time together."

While they argued, Teagan scrambled to remember the words the Princess had used back in the city.

"We didn't break them," she said in wonder. But when she looked over, she realized they weren't listening to her. "Hey!" They turned to her, and the Princess's expression was smug.

"We didn't break your rules. You said we weren't allowed to touch when on the Road of Silence." Teagan gestured to the sky, knowing the Princess knew exactly how they'd gotten there in the first place. She'd been watching them this whole time, probably impatient to drag them back into her clutches. "We weren't on the road when it happened."

The Princess waved it away as if it were nothing. "A simple technicality."

"You promised!" Teagan yelled. "You gave your word! Does your word really mean nothing now?"

The Princess's eyes narrowed. "I could just feed you to the bones, let you rot here, seeing your home just beyond the arch and knowing you'll never be there again."

"But you won't," Teagan said. "Because, deep down, you have to admit that you have a soft spot for stories like ours. For *love* like ours." Her gaze went to Cress, who gave her a tentative, encouraging smile. "I've always believed in you, even after hearing of your darkest moments, Queen Amalaris."

She didn't say anything for a time, and Teagan could see the debate behind her eyes. Until, finally, something settled and the witch nodded.

"As you said, I gave my word." She stepped away from them, and Teagan let out a sob of relief. She could see the arch in the distance and home had never sounded so good to her than in that moment, when she thought she'd never see it again. "You won't have to fight anymore, so go. Back to your tiny house and quiet life. Your *insignificant* lives. The human time span is nothing compared to mine. I'll be here long after your bodies have rotted in the ground." The Princess's eyes gleamed. "Long after the two of you have gotten bored with each other and your love turns sour with hate."

Teagan would give anything for that quiet, insignificant life right about now. Nothing the Princess said changed that. She started toward the arch, when Cress halted them. She smiled sweetly. "And the rest of your promise?"

The Shadow Princess sent her a scathing look, but she gestured for Teagan to roll up her sleeve. The pulsing, angry

149

wound was horrible. The Princess placed her hands over the bite and spoke in the old language. When she was finished, the wound disappeared, leaving no scar.

"The poison is gone."

"And it'll never come back?" Teagan asked, tears in her eyes.

"Not as you shall live." She pursed her lips. "But I won't save you a second time, even if you travel the road again."

Teagan was already being given another chance. She wouldn't be greedy. "Thank you."

For the very last time, they walked through an arch side by side.

As they stepped on solid, Wystiran ground Cress screamed into the sky, tears of joy pouring down her cheeks. She twirled around and around, making Teagan dizzy. "We did it."

"Because of you," Teagan shouted back. She reached out for Cress but stopped herself, before she remembered they no longer had to fear touch. She ran her hands over Cress's face and down her arms, and Cress did the same. This was the first time they could freely touch each other in days, and Cress laughed as more tears came and Teagan wiped them away with her fingers.

"And because of you." Cress pressed her forehead to Teagan's. "I can't believe I get to have the life I've always wanted with you."

Teagan couldn't quite believe it either. She didn't know if she would, even years down the line, knowing that at any moment it could all be taken back. If the Princess truly wished it. But Teagan pushed these thoughts away, because here was the love of her life, safe and sound and whole. And they had all kinds of adventures waiting for them. "I'm never leaving you again," Cress whispered.

"You sure you didn't want to stay in that realm with the beautiful princess?" Teagan asked mischievously. "She seemed all too eager to keep you with her for all of eternity."

Cress laughed loudly, and then put her palm on Teagan's cheek, turning her to face her. "I've only eyes for you, love." Teagan couldn't wait anymore; she pressed her lips to Cress's, swallowing the sound of her delighted gasp. Cress kissed her back with the kind of fervor and desperation with which she'd thrown herself into the Shadow Realm. They collapsed in a tangled pile of limbs on the grass as the sun shone down on them.

They finally left the Hallowed Arch behind, not even sparing it a single look, and walked toward home, their arms entwined. Their giddiness hid their exhaustion and the pain from their bruises and scrapes. Giggling, Teagan covered Cress's face with tiny kisses. They were both so caught up in each other that they didn't pull apart until someone cleared their throat.

They broke away to find Maradin with her hands on her hips on her shop's stoop, an eyebrow arched in their direction. "So, you made it out, huh?"

They looked at each other, secret smiles on their faces. "We made it out," Cress said. "And we're never going back."

"It's good to see the two of you again," Maradin said with a smile. "Don't you make this a common occurrence."

"We'll try not to," Teagan replied before they headed off again.

When their house came into view, they ran toward it, breathless with happiness and excitement. Their cats mewled and ran circles around their legs, and as Cress gave Elra and Ohlia all the love and attention they demanded, Teagan went into their bedroom. She walked to the wooden chest on her bedside table. The one that had kept all of her most prized possessions safe over the years, the one that stored the images she had of her mother, and relics of the life Cress and her had shared together.

Teagan opened it with shaking fingers and picked up the letter she'd placed inside all those weeks ago, when she'd given up on her dreams.

It was time to chase them again.

Acknowledgements

Writing *The Bone Way* was a very whirlwind, solo endeavor for me, but I couldn't have done this without certain people. Thank you to my incredible best friends, Val and Rashika, who are always there for me and who pick me up when I'm down. And thank you to my awesome writer friends, Circe and Alyssa, who have been really supportive of my work. I'd also like to thank my mom, Carol, and brothers, Travis and Chad, for being there in the ways I need them. Lastly, many thanks to my editors, Celine, Hannah-Freya, and Rowan, for their insights and help in shaping this novella into a better story.

About the author

Holly J. Underhill was born into a family of writers and readers, so stories have always been a part of her life. She spends most of her time spinning tales about angry girls, queer acceptance, and mental health. She received a B.Sc. in psychology from Central Michigan University before she realized she wanted to be an author more than anything else. When not writing she enjoys finding new TV shows and books to fall in love with, nerding out over history, and going on adventures. She currently resides in Michigan with her family, one dog, and an abundance of rescue cats. *The Bone Way* is her first published work.